Just then Chet poked forward with his staff, catching Bo Reid solidly in the chest. Reid stumbled back and fell onto his rear end. Chet did a little victory dance, like a winning prizefighter. He didn't see Reid's staff swinging at his legs.

"Look out!" Frank called, too late.

Reid's blow swept Chet's feet out from under him, and the big teen stumbled back into one of the wide brick chimneys. Daphne gasped as Chet hit the mortar with a dull thud.

Willingham pulled out a referee's whistle and blew it. "Hold it!" he said. "That's enough!"

"I'm okay," Chet replied, pushing himself up off the chimney.

As he did, though, several of the bricks under his hands gave way. A low, rumbling groan filled the air. Chet looked up as the big chimney crumbled— right toward him.

S.2/5

The Hardy Boys Mystery Stories

Available from ALADDIN Paperbacks

THE HARDY BOYS®

#183
WAREHOUSE RUMBLE

FRANKLIN W. DIXON

Aladdin Paperbacks
New York London Toronto Sydney

This book is a work of fiction. Any references to historical events,
real people, or real locales are used fictitiously. Other names, characters, places,
and incidents are the product of the author's imagination,
and any resemblance to actual events or locales or persons, living or dead,
is entirely coincidental.

First Aladdin Paperbacks edition February 2004
Copyright © 2004 by Simon & Schuster, Inc.

ALADDIN PAPERBACKS
An imprint of Simon & Schuster
Children's Publishing Division
1230 Avenue of the Americas
New York, NY 10020

The text of this book was set in New Caledonia.

Printed in the United States of America
2 4 6 8 10 9 7 5 3

THE HARDY BOYS MYSTERY STORIES is a trademark of Simon & Schuster, Inc.

THE HARDY BOYS and colophon are registered trademarks of Simon & Schuster, Inc.

Library of Congress Control Number 2003105621

ISBN 0-689-86455-8

Contents

1 Contestants Wanted

"'The Great Contestant Hunt Continues'!" Chet Morton read the headline from the *Bayport Journal-Times* as though he were reciting Shakespeare. "'Ward Willingham, creator of the hit reality TV game show *Warehouse Rumble,* will be in Bayport this afternoon to interview prospective contestants for the show's pilot episode. . . .'"

"How can a TV show be a 'hit' if it they haven't even filmed the pilot yet?" Frank Hardy asked. The tall, dark-haired eighteen-year-old regarded both Chet and the newspaper skeptically.

"Maybe 'hit' is part of the title," Joe Hardy suggested. His blue eyes twinkled mischievously, and a broad grin spread across his handsome face. "You know, like Marvelous Marvin Haggler—who added

'Marvelous' to his legal name so announcers would use it when he entered the ring."

Iola Morton put down her forkful of salad and cocked an eyebrow at her boyfriend. "So, you're suggesting that the name of this show is *The Hit Reality TV Game Show: Warehouse Rumble*? That's a bit long, isn't it?"

Callie Shaw, who was sitting at the lunchroom table opposite her boyfriend, Frank, shrugged. "It could be true," she said. "TV people do strange things to get attention."

Daphne Soesbee, the pretty redhead sitting at Chet's elbow, pursed her lips in thought. "Ward Willingham was the producer of *TV's Greatest Cop Arrests*," she said. "That show was a hit. Maybe that's what the article means."

"So, if you have one hit show, then the next one is automatically a hit too?" Frank asked.

"Sneer if you want," Chet replied amiably. "But I think this could be our big chance."

Chet's sister, Iola, frowned. "Big chance for *what*?" she asked.

"Fame . . . fortune . . . all the usual stuff," Chet replied. He puffed up his chest, preened his sandy hair in movie star fashion, and shot the rest of the group a million-dollar smile. Chet had always dreamed of fame, and liked opportunities like this. "I'm gonna try out. Want to come with me, Daphne? The article says they need teams of two people."

"Sure," Daphne said, smiling. "After sitting out the Halloween contest that my mom ran, this might be a good chance to pick up a few bucks."

Joe took the paper from Chet. "It says here that the game is a treasure hunt that will involve both physical challenges and mental puzzles," he said.

Iola sighed. "Don't tell me *you're* falling for my brother's crazy scheme too?" she said. She tousled Joe's blond hair playfully.

"Hey, we're off from school for the rest of the week for teacher conferences," Joe said. "TV auditions sound like fun."

"I agree," Frank said. He finished his carton of milk and crumpled it with one hand. "Want a partner, bro? Or are you teaming up with Iola?"

"Oh no," Iola said. "Not me. I've got better things to do this week than humiliate myself on television."

"Me too," Callie added, smiling at Frank. "Iola and I promised to help out at the food pantry during our spare time. So you and your brother are free to run around like crazy men, trying to impress TV producers."

"Well, the trying-to-impress-TV-producers part would be new," Chet said, "but the running around like madmen—"

"How would anyone tell the difference?" Daphne asked, finishing his thought.

All four teens laughed.

Chet, Daphne, and the brothers decided to carpool out to the auditions after classes. They dropped off their school stuff at their homes, then headed for the address the newspaper had given for the show auditions.

Bayshore Road wound northeast from the center of town, past business offices and the waterfront park all the way to the old warehouse district on the north shore of Barmet Bay. The warehouses and factories lining the inlet were old and had fallen into disuse many years ago. Tall brick smokestacks still stretched crumbling fingers toward the sky, but no fires burned within any of them. The structures surrounding the chimneys still stood, though their brick walls were cracked and blackened, and Ivy had crept up many of the aging facades. Much of the translucent glass in the buildings' high, narrow windows was cracked and broken. Rotten holes showed through the wooden factory doors; the corroded metal doors of the warehouses hung askance.

The warehouses had been built early in the twentieth century to serve both the factories and the bayside docks that connected Bayport's industry to the world. The wharves behind structures looked as decrepit as the buildings themselves. Wide, concrete posts and slimy wooden piers jutted out of the water at crooked angles. Worm-eaten boards and crumbling concrete platforms rested atop the jumbled pylons. The wave-tossed waters of the bay clawed against the piers, threatening to finally drag them under.

Frank pulled the van off the main road and into the wide, dirt parking lot next to the building. A set of weed-clogged railroad tracks ran into the factory grounds from the north. The tracks looked every bit as abandoned as the warehouse itself.

Despite the setting's bleak appearance, more than a dozen cars—including a TV news van— lined the parking lot. Frank parked the car at the end of a row, and the four teens climbed out.

The Hardys and their friends hiked toward a sign on one of the warehouses that read CONTESTANTS WELCOME! They entered through a rusting metal door that appeared to have been repaired recently so it would hang right.

The interior of the building was no more impressive than the door. It was gray and dirty, with brick and cinder-block walls covered by crumbling plaster. The room they entered was large; its walls stood at least three stories tall and were capped by a corrugated-metal roof. A skeleton of rusting catwalks snaked through the air two stories up. Once, the gangways must have been used to service huge machines, but no trace of those machines remained.

The warehouse's high, narrow windows admitted only a bit of light, making the big room seem as though it were trapped in perpetual twilight. Fallen frames and plasterboard walls, broken masonry, and other rubble lay scattered around the floor.

Three big chimneys dominated the wide, open space on the right side of the room. They jutted up from the uneven wooden floor like massive brick pillars and thrust through the rusting roof overhead. Despite the shabbiness and disrepair, the sheer size of the place made it impressive.

A folding table had been set up next to the door where the teens entered the building. A well-dressed woman behind the table stood as they came in. "Here to try out?" she asked optimistically. The name tag on her lapel read JULIE KENDALL.

"Yep," Chet replied. The others nodded.

"Great," Ms. Kendall said. She gathered up four packets of photocopied sheets and handed one to each of the teens. "Here's some information about the show, as well as a confidentiality agreement, a sample contract . . . and a liability release, of course. You can join the other prospects by the refreshment table, read the papers over, then return them to me."

She pointed to a nearby makeshift waiting area. Folding chairs lined one wall. A table topped with a coffee machine, a hot chocolate dispenser, and doughnuts sat in the center. A number of other would-be contestants milled around the area, talking and sipping drinks.

"Mr. Willingham will explain the game and exactly what we're looking for in contestants in a few minutes," Ms. Kendall continued. "After he's finished speaking, we'll be happy to answer any questions you have."

"Thanks," Daphne said, looking over the stack of forms.

Ms. Kendall smiled. "Good luck making it on to the show."

The four teens headed for the waiting area as Ms. Kendall turned to greet another group of newcomers.

"Trouble," Joe said as they approached the coffee machine.

"Where?" Chet asked.

"Missy Gates and Jay Stone," Frank said, eyeing two teens leaning against the wall nearby.

Missy was short, thin, and had dyed-blond hair; Jay was tall and very lean, with dark hair and a sharp-featured face. Both of them wore beat-up jeans and black leather jackets with the word KINGS painted on the backs. The Kings were a "gang" of local punks who specialized in shady dealings—though neither Missy nor Jay had ever actually been arrested.

"We can handle them," Chet whispered to the rest. "We did last Halloween, right?"

"Hey!" Jay Stone called as he spotted the four friends. "If it ain't the Boy Scout Brothers and their twin sidekicks." He laughed, and Missy Gates snickered.

"Ignore them," Frank advised. "They're just looking to stir things up."

"Yeah," Joe agreed. "No sense getting kicked out of here before the auditions start."

The brothers, Chet, and Daphne got some drinks and doughnuts from the refreshment table and then found a spot on the folding chairs relatively far away from Missy and Jay. They read over the papers as they waited for the auditions to begin.

A dozen more people filtered into the waiting area over the next half hour. The Hardys didn't know any of them. A few talked with the others present, but most just stood in small, solitary groups, sipping their drinks and munching on doughnuts.

"Everybody's putting their game faces on," Joe whispered to the rest.

"Smart idea," Frank replied. "'Cause here comes the game-master."

Everyone looked up as a tall man with bushy brown hair walked into the room. He was as large as Chet, but not quite as stocky. He'd perched a pair of sunglasses on his nose, and was wearing a gold chain around his neck. A reporter with a microphone and two cameramen were covering the event. One of the cameramen had an ACTION NEWS logo on his equipment, the other had a camera with a UAN—United America Network—logo and the words WAREHOUSE RUMBLE roughly stenciled on the side.

Julie Kendall quickly got up from behind her table and fell into the short parade near the front. When the group stopped, she said, "Applicants, I'd like you to meet Ward Willingham, the producer and director of *Warehouse Rumble*."

She smiled, and everyone in the assembly applauded—all except Missy Gates and Jay Stone. They leaned against the wall, unimpressed.

Ward Willingham stepped between the cameras, smiled, and propped his beefy hands on his hips. "Hey, welcome!" he said. "Glad to see so many people here this afternoon to audition for *Warehouse Rumble!*" At this, he thrust his fists in the air enthusiastically, and the audience applauded. Some began whooping and cheering.

"That's the kind of homegrown enthusiasm that we've come to Bayport for!" Willingham said. "I know you're all pumped up to work on this smash hit with us—and we can't wait to see you strut your stuff.

"But first, let me tell you what the show is about. What you've read or heard about *Warehouse Rumble* doesn't begin to capture the thrill of the game itself!"

"Tell us about it!" Jay Stone called from the back of the crowd.

Joe and Frank thought he was heckling, but Ward Willingham didn't seem to care; his smile grew even wider. "*Warehouse Rumble* is a game that requires both strength and smarts. Teams will have to work together to compete and overcome obstacles. The game will have both physical challenges and mental puzzles. The awards will be amazing!"

9

Willingham paused a moment to let this idea sink in. "I can't reveal exactly what the prizes will be. I wouldn't want anyone who doesn't make the cut spilling our secrets to the media." He turned and winked at the cameras. "Besides, I doubt Bayport is ready to be the site of the next *gold rush.*"

An appreciative "Ooooh!" arose from the crowd.

"Do you think he means *real* gold?" Daphne whispered. Chet and the Hardys shrugged.

"To play *Warehouse Rumble,* you'll not only have to be smart and strong—you'll also have to be brave," Willingham continued. "There are monsters lurking in these old warehouses—at least, there *will* be after my crew is finished setting up." He smiled. "So anybody who's faint of heart better drop out now."

Willingham crossed his arms over his chest and surveyed the three dozen people in the crowd. No one looked like they were leaving. He smiled again.

"Good. Okay," he said. "If you read the literature, you know you need a team partner to play in this game. If any of you don't already have a partner, we'll try to pair you up with someone during the auditions. Right now, I need each of you to sign your release and liability forms, and turn them in to Ms. Kendall. Then I'll set you up with some sparring partners, and we can start the auditions."

"Sparring partners?" Daphne said skeptically. "I'm no wimp, but—"

Chet smiled at her. "Don't worry," he said, "I can spar enough for both of us."

"Let's get our paperwork turned in," Joe said, urging the four of them toward the rapidly forming line in front of Ms. Kendall's desk.

As the contestants turned in their forms, Willingham ushered the news crew out; he wanted only his own cameramen covering the auditions. A few minutes later he sent the Hardys and their friends to the far side of the warehouse, where a big practice arena had been set up. Gym mats covered the floor, and various pieces of athletic equipment stood ready to be used.

They spotted boxing gloves and bags, a balance beam, a makeshift broad-jump pit (with pads instead of sand), a hand-over-hand horizontal ladder, and a climbing board. There were long bamboo staffs, padded like punching bags, at either end of the area, and padded headgear sat nearby.

"I was never very good with a quarterstaff," Daphne told her friends.

"No problem," said Willingham, who was prowling through the area acting as impromptu trainer and judge. "Not every contestant has to pass every test. You pick the five you're most suited to, and we'll judge you on those. Each team has to pass at least four physical and four mental challenges. The remaining two are up to you."

"Sign me up," Chet said, hefting one of the padded staffs.

"Great," Willingham replied. "I'll find you a sparring partner."

Before either Frank or Joe could volunteer, Willingham motioned over a muscular guy with black, bowl-cut hair. His eyes narrowed when he saw the group. "Hey Daphne," he sneered. "Long time no see."

"Suit up," Willingham said, oblivious to the tension between the newcomer and Daphne. "Then start sparring." The new guy and Chet donned their headgear and took their places on the sparring mat near one of the old chimneys.

"Who's the big guy?" Joe whispered to Daphne.

"Bo Reid," Daphne replied. "He and I were rivals back when I played Creature Cards—the collectible card game—a lot. I beat him regularly in tournaments. He doesn't like me much. I hope he doesn't take it out on Chet."

"Chet can handle himself," Frank said.

They stepped back and watched as Bo and Chet squared off. Though neither contestant had much experience, they more than made up for it with enthusiasm—dodging and swinging, and generally trying to pound each other into the mat.

"Great! Great!" Willingham yelled every time he looked in their direction.

Chet and Bo redoubled their efforts, and soon

12

sweat was pouring off their brows. Two of the staff cameramen came over to cover the event, and many of the other contestants—including Missy Gates and Jay Stone—looked on enviously.

"I think your team's place on the show is cinched," Joe whispered to Daphne.

Frank nodded his agreement. "Willingham would be a fool to turn away either of these guys. They're putting on a great show."

Just then Chet poked forward with his staff, catching Bo Reid solidly in the chest. Reid stumbled back and fell onto his rear end. Chet did a little victory dance, like a winning prizefighter. He didn't see Reid's staff swinging at his legs.

"Look out!" Frank called, too late.

Reid's blow swept Chet's feet out from under him, and the big teen stumbled back into one of the wide brick chimneys. Daphne gasped as Chet hit the mortar with a dull thud.

Willingham pulled out a referee's whistle and blew it. "Hold it!" he said. "That's enough!"

"I'm okay," Chet replied, pushing himself up off the chimney.

As he did, though, several of the bricks under his hands gave way. A low, rumbling groan filled the air. Chet looked up as the big chimney crumbled—right toward him.

2 Bricks and Stones . . .

"Chet!" Daphne screamed as a huge section of the chimney collapsed toward the startled teen.

Joe and Frank sprinted forward to help their friend.

Still dazed, Chet staggered as pieces of crumbling brick pelted him.

Ignoring the falling masonry, the Hardys rushed in and grabbed Chet, one under each arm. The collapse kicked up a huge cloud of dust, making it difficult to see or breathe. The brothers backpedaled as quickly as they could, dragging Chet out of the falling debris. As they left, bricks continued raining onto the floor of the deserted factory.

"Phew!" Joe said as the collapse finally stopped.

Frank brushed pieces of crumbled brick out of his dark hair. "I think it's over," he said. Most of the six-foot-wide chimney remained standing, but there was a big hole in the side of it. The breach looked like a mouth yawning into an inky abyss.

"Thanks, guys," Chet said groggily.

Daphne waded into the cloud of settling dust. "Are you all okay?" she asked.

"We're fine," Joe replied.

"Just a few bumps and bruises," Chet added. He smiled and gave Daphne a reassuring hug.

Bo Reid, the cameramen, and the others who had gathered to watch the "joust" kept moving back. They coughed up dust and waved their hands to clear the air.

"Is anyone hurt?" Ward Willingham asked.

The crowd shook their heads, and most of them mumbled, "No."

Willingham walked over to Chet, eyeing the big teen carefully. "You didn't crack your head or anything, did you?" he asked, brushing some of the dust off of Chet's clothes.

Chet shook his head. "Nope. I'm fine."

"Good," Willingham replied, forcing a smile. "No need to get the insurance company involved, then."

From the back of the crowd, Jay Stone called, "Ow! I twisted my ankle!" He bent down and clutched his leg.

Willingham looked sternly at him.

"Just kidding," Stone said. "I was just hamming it up for the show."

Willingham nodded slowly, but his dark sunglasses didn't look too forgiving. Turning to his cameramen, he asked, "Did you catch the accident on film?"

One dust-covered man shook his head, but the woman running the other camera gave a grin and a thumb's-up.

"Great," Willingham replied, breaking into his Hollywood smile again. "That could be a super promo."

Frank frowned. "Chet could have been hurt."

"But he wasn't," Willingham replied, putting his arm around Chet's shoulder. "And it was *great* TV. But don't anyone else try anything like that." He paused for a moment. "Okay, everybody back to work."

"We should move the auditions across the ware-house," Julie Kendall said, "so a crew can clean up this mess."

"Right," Willingham agreed. "Everybody, grab some equipment and move it over there." He pointed to the far side of the big room. "We'll keep auditions going. We only have a limited amount of time before shooting starts, and I want to see every one of you work." He turned to Chet. "You can take five. You're in."

"What about me?" Bo Reid asked.

16

"You too, big guy. Grab some coffee and a doughnut. I know you both have what it takes for *Warehouse Rumble*."

"How about our partners?" Chet asked.

"Nobody's a shoo-in," Willingham said, "but they've got a leg up on the rest." He turned to Daphne. "Pick an event and show me what you've got."

Daphne nodded.

"Okay, let's go!" he said, leading the rest of the contestants to the far side of the warehouse.

"See you later, Daphne," Bo Reid said menacingly. He turned and headed for the coffee machine.

"Maybe you will," Daphne shot back.

"Well," Chet said jauntily, "that was easy,"

"For *you*, maybe," Daphne replied. "I nearly had a heart attack. You're sure you're all right?"

"Never been righter," Chet said. "I'm gonna grab some grub before that Reid character hogs it all."

"Those of us without a free pass better get back to the auditions," Joe said. He winked in Chet's direction.

"What do you think they'll do if one of us doesn't make the cut?" Daphne asked.

"Probably re-pair us up with different contestants," Frank replied.

"I'm sure you'll all make it," Chet said confidently. See you later." He headed for the doughnuts while the Hardys and Daphne rejoined the other prospective contestants.

The brothers and Daphne moved quickly through a series of tests. All of them did well on the puzzles. Daphne aced the balance beam, while the brothers did well on the climbing and swinging challenges. By the time they took their next scheduled break, all three of them had worked up a good sweat.

"How're you doing?" Chet asked.

"Good," Daphne replied, wiping the perspiration from her forehead.

"All of you look great out there," Chet said. "Willingham would have to be a dunce not to pick you."

"Something tells me that brains and TV production don't always go together," Joe said.

At that moment the front door flew open, and a short, balding man with a hawkish nose and frizzy brown hair stalked in. He was wearing a brown three-piece suit, and sweating uncomfortably in it. His face grew red as he approached Willingham. "What's this I hear about an accident?" he asked angrily.

Ms. Kendall tried to cut the man off, but Willingham stepped around her and faced the visitor. "Mr. Jackson . . . ," Ward Willingham began, ". . . Herman . . . buddy, don't worry. If it had been a real problem, we would have notified you right away."

"I was actually going to call you during this break," Ms. Kendall said.

"Did any of your contestants get hurt?" Herman Jackson asked.

"Oh no," Willingham said. "There was just a minor problem with one of the old chimneys."

The smaller Jackson craned his neck to see around Willingham's big frame. "*Minor* problem?" he said, spotting the hole in the chimney and the pile of rubble next to it. "It looks like a disaster! You promised me that none of the warehouse would be damaged."

"That's not precisely true," Ms. Kendall said, checking some papers on her clipboard. "Our contract stipulates that portions of the warehouse and grounds that are scheduled for demolition are exempt. We can alter them as we like."

"Including tearing them down," Willingham added with a smile. "See? There's nothing really to worry about here."

"Nothing except destroying Bayport's heritage!" shouted a voice from near the warehouse door.

Everyone in the room turned to see a lanky, blond man with a bushy mustache. He took a few steps toward Willingham and Jackson.

"What are *you* doing here?" Jackson asked, dismayed.

"You can't keep the public out when you're

planning to demolish a valuable historical site!" the blond man said.

"Is this the guy you warned me about?" Willingham asked Jackson.

"Yes," Jackson replied. "Clark Hessmann. Local crusading nutcase."

Ms. Kendall stepped between Clark Hessmann and her boss. "Mr. Hessmann," she said calmly, "you know you're *not* supposed to be here."

"I'm here to try out," Hessmann snapped. "This audition is open to the public, isn't it?"

"Only during specific hours," Willingham called at him. "You're too late to try out today."

"And I've got a restraining order against you," Jackson added.

"So what?" Hessmann shot back. "I'm more than fifty feet away from you."

"That pertains to the outdoors," Jackson said. "You're not supposed to be in the same building as me. Not unless it's a public place."

"This is a public audition, so it's a public place," Hessmann replied.

"I'm sorry, Mr. Hessmann," Julie Kendall said. "Auditions are closed for the night. I'm going to have to ask you to leave."

Two of Willingham's security people—who had been helping clean up the rubble—jogged toward the activist.

Hessmann backed toward the door. "All right, I'm

going," he said. "But I'll be back. You can't keep me out! The people have a right to know!" He exited the warehouse before the guards could escort him out.

Ms. Kendall, Willingham, and Jackson all breathed a sigh of relief as security closed the door behind him.

"That was . . . interesting," Joe whispered to Frank. The elder Hardy merely nodded.

"I'll talk to my lawyer," Jackson said quietly to Willingham, "and try to keep him off the property."

"Good idea," Willingham agreed.

Nearly everyone in the warehouse had gathered near the exit to watch the commotion. "Everything's under control here," Willingham told them. "Nothing to worry about. Everyone can get back to work. I'll be continuing my judging in just a few minutes."

Most of the hopeful contestants went back to work. A few, though, hung around to see if there would be any more fireworks.

"Now, about the chimney collapse . . . ?" Jackson asked Willingham. He was much more calm now than he had been when he'd first entered the warehouse. He mopped his balding head with a white handkerchief.

"Don't worry, Jack," Missy Gates quipped. "No one *important* got hurt."

Herman Jackson sputtered. "N-no one *important . . . ?*"

"Relax, Herman," Willingham said, putting his arm around the smaller man's shoulder. "She's just pulling your leg. Aren't you?" He shot Missy a nasty look. She shrugged and went back to the auditions.

"I was next to the chimney when it collapsed," Chet said. "I didn't get hurt much."

"*Much?*" Jackson said, still alarmed.

"Just a few bruises and some dirty clothes," Joe explained.

Jackson let out a long sigh of relief. "Well, if that's all . . ."

"Stop worrying," Willingham said. "You'll live longer. Trust me. Now, why don't you just head home and dream about all the publicity *Warehouse Rumble* is going to generate for you when you sell this dump?"

"Okay," Jackson said, nodding. "I'm sorry I overreacted. Next time, though, make sure you call me *immediately.*"

"Herman, there won't *be* a next time," Willingham said sincerely. He walked Jackson toward the door, talking quietly to the man as they went.

"Where are you five supposed to be?" Ms. Kendall asked. She looked at Bo Reid, the Hardys, and their friends and checked her clipboard.

"Me and lardo got a free pass," Reid called from nearby.

"That's *Mister* Lardo to you, chump," Chet shot back.

"We're on break," Frank said quickly, trying to defuse things before Chet and Reid could start up again.

"Ah, yes," Ms. Kendall said. "Enjoy your time off. Mr. Willingham wants you back at practice in ten minutes." She flipped her papers closed and walked away.

"I'm hitting the bathroom," Daphne said. "Did any of you notice where it is?"

"On the far side of the warehouse," Chet replied.

"Past the chimneys," Frank added.

Daphne jogged off in that direction while the Hardys grabbed some hot cocoa and doughnuts. Bo Reid sneered at them and then moved away to watch some of the auditions.

"Nice guy," Joe said, clearly meaning just the opposite.

"Too bad the chimney didn't fall on *him*," Frank added.

Just then, a piercing scream rose above the clamor of the warehouse.

The Hardys and Chet turned and saw Daphne standing stock-still near the broken chimney. Her eyes were wide, and her skin looked very pale.

The brothers and Chet sprinted to her side.

"What's wrong?" Frank asked.

Daphne pointed to the bottom of the pile of broken bricks lying next to the chimney.

Poking out of the rubble was a skeletal hand.

3 . . . May Break Old Bones

The Hardys and their friends stared at the bony fingers that were protruding from beneath the wreckage of the old chimney.

"What's happening? Is anybody hurt?" Ward Willingham called as he rushed to the scene.

"This guy definitely doesn't look well," Chet said.

"But I don't think the trouble is very recent," Frank added grimly.

Daphne shook her head. "It *couldn't* be one of the contestants."

"Not unless piranhas live in these chimneys," said Joe.

"What do you mean?" Willingham asked. He

stopped when he spotted the skeletal hand. The other people in the warehouse began to gather around the chimney as well.

"Keep back," Julie Kendall said. "It might not be safe."

"Is this some kind of prank?" Willingham asked angrily. He looked around until he found the crew who had been working on removing the rubble. "Do you guys know anything about this?"

The cleanup crew merely shrugged and shook their heads.

"All right," Willingham said, "everyone back to work. We're on a tight schedule here. We don't have a lot of time to waste."

"You *have* to call the police on this," Frank said. "Even if it turns out to be just a prank."

Willingham glared, then finally said, "All right. Julie, get the police on the phone, would you?"

Julie Kendall pulled out her cell phone and dialed 911.

"We should keep everyone away from the skeleton," Joe suggested.

"How about we start with you guys," Willingham snapped. He waved his hands at the Hardys and their friends, indicating they should move toward the other side of the warehouse.

The teens, the other contestants, and the members of the crew moved away from the chimneys. A number of contestants, including Daphne, took the opportunity to visit the bathroom.

"The police are on their way," Ms. Kendall announced as she snapped her cell phone shut.

"Good," Willingham said, though he didn't seem to mean it. "Let's try to get in some more practice before they arrive."

Slowly, the prospective contestants drifted back to their routines. As they did, a loud knock sounded on the door.

"That's awfully fast," Ms. Kendall said, indicating to one member of her crew to open the door.

The crewman did, and two people bustled inside. The one in front was a well-dressed woman holding a microphone. Behind her came a man holding a TV camera with the letters WSDS stenciled on the side.

"Stacia Allen, WSDS News," announced the woman. "What's going on here?"

"Nothing," Willingham said, smiling awkwardly. "We're holding tryouts for *Warehouse Rumble*."

"The reality-game pilot that's shooting in Bayport?" Ms. Allen asked, sticking her microphone in front of Willingham. "Are you the show's producer?"

"Yes," Willingham replied. He lowered his sunglasses, and his eyes narrowed. "Aren't you from a news magazine on a rival network? I don't remember issuing credentials to your crew."

"How did these news hawks get here before the police?" Chet whispered to the Hardys.

"Maybe they were listening in on the police radio band," Joe suggested.

"Or they could have been on their way here *before* the call went out to the police," Frank said.

"You're thinking that Hessmann guy called them?" Joe asked.

"He said people had a right to know what was going on here," Frank said.

"If that's the case," Chet replied, "this news crew is going to get a much better story than they bargained for."

Ms. Kendall stepped up next to her boss. "WSDS wasn't issued credentials, sir," she said to Willingham.

"You don't need credentials to follow up on a news story," Stacia Allen said. "I hear there's some hot news in this warehouse tonight. Care to comment?"

"*Warehouse Rumble* is going to be the hottest new show of the season," Willingham said, falling into his rehearsed patter. He tried to position himself between the TV camera and the broken chimney.

"That's not what I'm talking about," Ms. Allen said. "What can you tell me about this accident?" She and her cameraman tried to move around Willingham toward the chimneys.

"That's a matter for the police," Frank said, stepping in front of her.

Ms. Allen glared at him. "Who are you?" she

asked. "What's your relationship to this program?"

"Frank Hardy. I'm just one of the people trying out for the show."

Allen's eyebrows raised. "The son of Fenton Hardy, the detective? And that must be your younger brother, Joe."

"Guilty," Joe said, stepping up beside his brother.

"So you really don't have any authority to stop us," Ms. Allen said, trying to outflank the Hardys.

"They don't, but *we* do," said a voice from the doorway.

The brothers turned and saw Officers Con Riley and Gus Sullivan, two of Bayport's finest, standing in the door.

"Looks like we got here just in time," Sullivan continued. He was older than Riley, but Riley outranked him.

"You should know better than to try to disturb a crime scene, Ms. Allen," Riley said. Riley and Officer Sullivan walked up to the group and barred the way of the news crew.

"Crime scene . . . ?" Allen said. For a moment, her eyes lit up at the discovery, then she recovered her composure. "Since when is shooting pictures interfering with the police? The press have rights, you know."

"So do the police," Officer Sullivan countered.

"So do *I*," Willingham put in. He shook hands with the police and introduced himself. "This is the

28

set of *my* TV show. I won't have rival networks poking around."

"Ever hear of the First Amendment?" Stacia Allen asked.

"Let's not get worked up," Con Riley said. "She *does* have the right to cover news, and if you've really found a skeleton in that chimney, that would qualify."

Ms. Allen shot Willingham a smug grin.

"However, we'll try to keep her out of your hair," Riley finished.

"But I'm holding auditions here!" Willingham said.

Julie Kendall sidled up to her boss. "Maybe we should call it a day," she suggested. "We've got another session scheduled for the morning. These people could come back and finish their auditions then."

"That sounds like a good idea," Riley said.

"Yeah, okay," Willingham agreed. "Everybody head for home. Auditions resume at nine A.M.—sharp—tomorrow morning."

"If you've witnessed the trouble here, please stay so Officer Sullivan can interview you," Con Riley added.

"I'm doing interviews as well," Stacia Allen announced, "after the police are through, of course." She shot Con Riley a condescending smile.

"Just stay out of our way," Riley said. He turned toward the Hardys. "Good to see you kids again.

Do you have any information about this?"

"We'll be happy to tell you what we know," Joe said. Daphne had returned from the bathroom. She, Frank, and Chet nodded their agreement.

"Great," the officer said. "Talk to Sullivan. I have to take a statement from Mr. Willingham." He and Willingham walked toward the broken chimney.

Stacia Allen tried to follow, but Sullivan cut her off. "You'll get your chance," he said. "Later."

More police arrived to help with the crime scene, but the interviews still went slowly. The cops kept the newspeople at bay as long as they could, though Ms. Allen and her cameraman managed to get some shots of the broken chimney and the skeleton beneath it.

Ward Willingham decided to give the WSDS crew an interview after all. He kept talking about the game; Allen tried to steer him toward the "accident."

It was nearly midnight by the time the Hardys and their friends arrived home. They all went straight to bed and quickly fell asleep.

The four friends assembled in the Hardys' kitchen early the next morning. Frank made pancakes while Joe handled the eggs and bacon. Daphne and Chet set the table and poured drinks. A radio on the counter blared the news and weather.

Frank paged through the morning paper as they ate. "They discovered whose skeleton it was," Frank announced. "He had I.D. in what was left of his clothing. His name was Joss Orlando. He used to live in Bayport."

"I heard on the radio that he'd been missing for fifteen years," Daphne said.

"I thought he looked a little thin," Joe added sardonically.

"How did he get in the chimney?" Chet asked.

"They think he fell in from the roof," Frank said. "But why was he up there?" He shrugged.

"Con Riley and the cops will figure it out eventually," Joe said.

"Well, I'm glad this is one mystery the *police* get to solve," Daphne said, winking at the brothers.

Chet looked at his watch. "You guys need to be getting to the auditions," he said.

"I'm surprised you didn't sleep in—since you've already earned a spot on the show," Joe said.

"Hey, I've got to root for my friends, don't I?" Chet asked.

"Great—let's get going, then," Frank said, putting his dishes in the washer.

They finished cleaning up, then piled into the Hardys' van and drove out to the old warehouse. Ms. Kendall greeted them as they entered. The refreshment area had been moved to the other side of the warehouse, away from the crime scene, which now had yellow police tape around it. A number of local news crews were poking around, including Stacia Allen and her cameraman.

They saw quite a few new faces among the crowd waiting to try out, though the overall group wasn't much bigger than the one the day before.

"It looks like some people from yesterday didn't come back," Chet said.

"Too bad Bo Reid wasn't one of them," Daphne noted, spotting the big, black-haired teen chatting with Missy and Jay near the wall.

"He has a guaranteed place in the show," Joe said. "He'd be a dope to drop out. I wonder where the others are, though?"

Joe shrugged. "Maybe the tryouts were too rough for them."

"Or maybe they didn't like the decor," Frank suggested.

"I wasn't going to come," said a girl standing nearby. She had stringy, blond-streaked black hair and was dressed all in black, Goth-style. "That chimney accident sounded way dangerous."

"This whole place is falling apart," commented her companion. He was a bit taller than Frank and Chet and was decked out in black clothes like the girl.

"Then I thought," the girl continued, "it would be pretty radical to be on TV—even the local news. I'm Lily Sabatine. This is my brother, Todd. We're trying out." She and the tall teen shook hands with the group.

"Don't let my sister fool you," Todd said. "She digs danger."

Lily laughed. "Busted! C'mon, Todd, let's see how close we can get to that police tape."

"Hmm . . . a little morbid?" Daphne asked as the siblings left.

"Danger is bread and butter to some people," Frank said.

"Coffee and doughnuts to others," Chet added with a grin at the Hardys.

"Looks like your boyfriend is cornering the doughnuts," someone said to Daphne.

The four friends turned and saw Bo Reid lurking nearby, a smirk on his face.

"What's the matter, Reid?" Chet asked. "Couldn't win at Creature Cards, so you've made acting like a sore loser your hobby?"

"Maybe I just don't like snotty redheads who hang around with fat slobs," Reid shot back.

Chet balled up his fists and stepped forward. "Maybe you should mind your own business before I topple you on your can again."

"Try it," Reed countered. He clenched his fists and came at Chet.

Frank stepped between the two of them, trying to head off the confrontation.

As he did, though, Bo Reid clouted the elder Hardy on the back of the head.

4 One Good Punch Deserves Another

The sudden attack surprised Frank more than hurt him. His martial arts training enabled him to roll with the blow. He somersaulted forward and came up on his feet once more, ready for action.

"Out of the way, you!" Reid said, aiming a punch at Frank's face.

Frank ducked aside and counterattacked. He smashed the heel of his palm squarely onto Reid's chin. Reid staggered back, blinking in surprise.

Chet and Joe rushed forward to help, but Frank said, "Stay back. I can handle this loudmouth."

Reid came at him again, feinting with his left and then bringing a hard right toward Frank's gut. Frank turned away from the punch and brought a karate chop down on Reid's left shoulder. Reid lumbered forward into some empty folding chairs.

Frank assumed a defensive martial arts stance. "Had enough?" he asked.

Bo Reid shoved the chairs aside and whirled to face the elder Hardy. Reid's black bowl-cut hair look like an unkempt mop; his eyes blazed with anger. With an incoherent grunt, he charged, throwing his arms wide to tackle Frank.

The dark-haired Hardy dropped and whirled in a spin kick. He swept Reid's legs out from under him. Frank's beefy opponent crashed hard to the floor.

A whistle blew loudly. "What's all this commotion?" Ward Willingham asked as he pushed through the crowd that had gathered to watch the fight. "There's no sparring in this area."

"Reid thought he'd get in a little extra falling practice," Chet said.

Bo Reid rubbed his chin as he rose; Frank maintained his defensive posture. "These guys tried to jump me," Reid said, indicating the Hardys and Chet.

"That's a lie!" Daphne said. "Reid threw the first punch."

Willingham frowned, pushed his sunglasses down on his nose, and glared at everyone gathered in the area. "Look," he said, "I don't know what kind of grudges some of you may have against one another—and I don't care. When you come onto *my* set, leave your petty squabbles at the door.

"Being tough rivals during the game is fine. In

between takes, though, you'd better make nice with one another. If you can't do that, you can't be on *Warehouse Rumble*. I don't have the time or money to put up with troublemakers.

"Anyone screwing around will be out on the street in a nanosecond—whether you've passed your auditions or not. Do I make myself clear?" Willingham looked around the crowd, warning everyone nearby.

"Crystal clear," Frank replied.

"Yeah, okay," Reid said.

Joe, Chet, Daphne, and the rest of the crowd mumbled their agreement.

"You're not throwing them out of the auditions?" Stacia Allen asked. She and her cameraman had pushed to the front of the crowd. The other reporters also had their cameras on the scene.

"Kick them out for what?" Willingham asked, suddenly becoming all smiles. "Youthful high spirits? *Warehouse Rumble* is *about* intensity."

"Okay," he continued after soaking up the spotlight for a moment, "everyone, back to work." He hooked his thumb toward the audition testing stations. As the crowd dispersed Willingham pulled Reid aside. "You get me, hotshot?" he asked.

Reid nodded.

"And you," Willingham said, pointing at Frank, "Mr. Karate, save your chops for the auditions. You're going to need them."

"No problem," Frank replied.

Stacia Allen stuck her microphone toward Frank's face, but Willingham deflected it and herded her and the other reporters away. "You can talk to the kids after the auditions if you want," the producer said. "For now, I need them concentrating on the game. Now . . . let me tell you more about *Warehouse Rumble*. . . ." He paused only long enough to shoo Lily and Todd Sabatine away from the crime scene perimeter.

"This ain't over, freaks," Reid called as he walked away.

"Anytime," Frank replied.

Daphne let out a long sigh of relief. "You know," she said, "I think that Ward Willingham was actually *pleased* about the fight. He was trying not to smile the whole time he lectured us."

"He's a real publicity hound," Joe said. "After bawling Stacia Allen out yesterday, he's still letting her snoop around the show."

"Speaking of which," Chet said, "you guys better get back to the auditions if you want to make the cut. They're picking finalists between now and lunch."

Joe nodded. "Wish us luck."

"Break a leg," Chet replied.

Frank, Joe, and Daphne went back to the tests. Because this was their second day and they didn't need to prove themselves that much more, they quickly completed their remaining tasks and soon rejoined Chet in the refreshment area.

The auditions wrapped up just after noon, and it took Willingham and his crew about forty-five minutes to make the final cuts. The *Warehouse Rumble* team thanked everyone who had tried out, then announced the names of the people who would be competing on the show.

The Hardys and Daphne joined Chet and Bo Reid on the final list. So did the Sabatines, Missy Gates, and Jay Stone, among numerous others. Thirty-two contestants were finally selected. Each day of shooting, some teams would be eliminated.

"All right!" Willingham said, flashing a big Hollywood smile. "Most of you already have partners for the competition. Those of you who don't should check with Ms. Kendall. She's got a list of the pairings. The final preparations and briefing will take thirty minutes. Then we'll begin the first contest."

"Our staff will go over the rules with each group of teams," Ms. Kendall added.

"I want to congratulate all of you for making it this far," Willingham continued. "Now comes the fun part. I want you to play fair, and play hard. Let's all work together to make *Warehouse Rumble* the hit I *know* it's going to be!"

"Hey," Joe whispered, "I thought we were a hit *already*."

Julie Kendall took the Hardys and their friends, along with four other contestants, aside to brief them and answer questions. Willingham and the rest of the staff briefed the other contestants.

"*Warehouse Rumble* is set in the future," Ms. Kendall said. "The world is a wasteland, and resources are scarce. Teams of adventurers wander the countryside in search of fortune. On their quests they'll have to overcome numerous obstacles, as well as combat other teams and the monstrous mutants that lurk in the ruins of the old civilization."

"Sounds like a fun place," said Chet. His friends and the rest of the contestants laughed.

Ms. Kendall smiled. "It'll make fun TV, that's for sure. We have team T-shirts for each of you 'Rumblers' to wear. You can customize your outfits if you like by adding accessories—but we *must* be able to see your team colors at all times. The TV audience needs to know who you're playing for—and against. Remember, this is supposed to be a grungy future."

"Like the *Road Warrior*," Frank said.

"Exactly. Throughout the challenges there will be treasure for you to discover—so keep your eyes peeled for them. Securing the final treasures will determine who wins the Warehouse Rumble." Ms. Kendall paused and looked around the group. "Any questions?" She looked around; no one looked confused. "No? Good. Get costumed up, and then meet near the refreshment area for your first assignments. You can use the bathrooms at the far end of the warehouse to change."

As the group broke up Chet said, "The Sabatines will fit right in with this scenario. No costumes necessary."

"Maybe they'll be given bright pink costumes," Daphne mused, smiling.

"That'd really compliment their Goth look," Joe quipped.

Ten minutes later all the teams assembled once more. Some had taken the time to work on their costumes, while others looked more or less normal. Daphne chose to wear her leather jacket over her team colors; Chet wore his Bayport High jacket. Frank and Joe both slicked down their hair and rolled up the sleeves of their T-shirts. Both Bo Reid and his partner, a buff, redheaded kid the Hardys didn't know, had torn their shirts in strategic places. The Sabatines wore their T-shirts like bandannas; they looked very postapocalyptic.

Willingham allowed the TV cameras to get a look at the assembled contestants. Then he ushered everyone but his own crew out of the warehouse. After a final rousing pep talk, he sent the teams off to compete in the different events set up throughout the abandoned warehouse complex. Daphne and Chet headed out to the old docks, while Frank and Joe remained inside.

The Hardys' first challenge was a relay race through a maze-like obstacle course, that had been constructed from fallen girders and other broken pieces of the old building. Frank, being slightly thinner, elected to take the first leg—which involved squeezing through some tight places. Joe would finish up the second leg, which required pushing through obstacles and confronting another contestant.

"It'd be nice if we knew who we were competing against," Frank said as he and Joe set up at one end of the course.

"Don't sweat it," Joe replied. "Whoever it is, we'll come out on top."

A member of the staff gave Frank a baton with a glowing lightstick inside it, then took Joe out of sight to the place where he'd begin his leg of the race.

Frank set himself into position and waited for the Klaxon signal to start. When it came, he sprinted off the starting line. He dodged between two "fallen walls"—actually fakes, constructed by the show's crew—and then squeezed through a half-open metal door.

As he ran he caught a glimpse of someone moving through the parallel course to his right. It was the buff, red-haired kid—Bo Reid's partner.

Frank gritted his teeth and surged forward through the remaining obstacles. He crawled under one last girder and handed the glowing baton to Joe. "You're facing Reid," he said, gasping for breath.

Joe's blue eyes gleamed at the prospect. He bulled his way through the first challenge: a set of hanging punching bags that bumped into one another like a series of swinging walls.

He sprinted up a slick incline, and then a swung on a rope over a pit. Joe guessed that the cameras wouldn't see the thick, dark cushions in the bottom of the pit—placed there in case he lost his grip. Next, he shoved aside some heavy "columns" made of chicken wire, plaster, and paint.

Forging ahead, Joe came to another pit. This one had a rope net stretched over the top of it. There was an entrance onto the net on either side of the course, but only one way off, at the far end.

Joe could see the finish line just beyond the netting. At the same time, he spotted Bo Reid at the other entrance.

Both of them lurched onto the net, toward the exit at the far side. As they struggled forward, it became obvious that they'd have to battle each other to reach the exit.

"I got a message for your brother and Morton," Reid hissed. "The word is . . . *pain*! Too bad it's your turn to play delivery boy."

"I think I'll mark this one 'Return to sender,'" Joe quipped. He and Reid now stood less than ten feet apart.

Suddenly the doors to the warehouse burst open. Someone with a megaphone yelled, "Hold it! Stop everything!"

5 Flack from the Flack

Willingham's security rushed toward the front entrance as Clark Hessmann and a well-dressed woman strode into the warehouse. Julie Kendall hurried to cut them off. "You can't come in here!" she sputtered.

"This paper says we can," Hessmann replied, holding out a piece of white parchment with printing on it.

"It's a restraining order," said the well-dressed woman. "I'm Helen Scott, Mr. Hessmann's lawyer."

"This paper says you've got to stop filming in Jackson's warehouse," Hessmann said proudly.

Ward Willingham blew his referee's whistle and yelled, "Cut! Cut! Everybody take five until we can figure this out." He hurried over to where the guards had converged on Hessmann and his lawyer.

The members of the crew stationed around the warehouse put down their cameras and relaxed.

Joe Hardy and Bo Reid eyed each other across the short expanse of rope netting that separated them. "You got lucky this time, Hardy," Reid said. "No way I'm tussling with you off-camera."

"Nice excuse," Joe shot back. "Maybe next time something else will come up to save you."

Reid went red in the face but said nothing more. Instead he went to the far side of the course and lowered himself off the net and onto the ground. Frank met Joe as the younger Hardy did the same.

"Glad you're okay," Frank said.

"I could have taken him," Joe replied.

"I know. Let's see what all this commotion is about." Frank and Joe joined the crowd that had gathered around Hessmann and Willingham. Daphne and Chet arrived a few moments later.

"This is ludicrous," Willingham was saying.

"The court believes that filming in this warehouse may be hazardous to your cast and crew," Scott replied.

"We've got all the proper permits," Willingham argued. "We have permission of the buildings' owner. We have a legal right to be here."

"Not until a cause of death is determined for the corpse of Joss Orlando," Hessmann said. "He could have been killed by toxic waste, for all you know.

You could be shooting this show in a toxic-waste dump."

"That's absurd," Julie Kendall said. "There are no records of toxic materials ever being used in this factory."

"What about in the years it's been shut down? Who knows what might have been stored here," Hessmann said. "Not to mention the fact that the building's unsafe. Part of that chimney collapsed the other day." He pointed to the big hole where they'd found the skeleton.

"You're just doing this because you have a problem with Herman Jackson," Willingham said accusingly.

"It's true," Hessmann replied, "that Jackson and I don't see eye to eye. He wants to tear down this historic warehouse district and destroy a vital link to Bayport's past. But that has nothing to do with this court order."

Willingham was fuming. "That's a cheap ploy, Hessmann. Jackson has got a right to do what he wants with his property—and that includes letting me film here before his demolition teams flatten this whole block."

"This writ says otherwise," Scott said.

"Well, we'll see what my lawyer and Jackson's have to say about that," Willingham replied. He pulled a cell phone out of his pocket and began dialing.

"Everybody take another five—we'll need a little time to sort this out," Ms. Kendall said, trying to disperse the crowd.

Joe elbowed Frank. "Looks like the news vultures sneaked in during the commotion." He pointed to a spot near the door where Stacia Allen and her cameraman were standing. They crept closer and began interviewing people as Hessmann and Willingham continued bickering.

"I think she's getting as much publicity out of this as Willingham is," Frank said.

"She builds up her own network show while dragging Willingham down," Daphne added, nodding.

"It's a win-win situation for WSDS," Chet admitted.

Julie Kendall noticed Allen and moved to intercept her.

"Looks like a second front is opening up," Joe said.

"It's a whole *new* rumble," Daphne joked.

Frank nodded. "Let's get something to drink," he said. "No telling how long this may go on, and I'm betting they'll want to get right back to shooting as soon as they figure things out."

"*If* they figure this out," Chet said.

"I've got a court order countermanding your order on the way," Willingham said as he hung up the phone.

"But our court order is here now," Scott said. "You can't go on shooting while it's in effect."

"We'll see what the police say about that," Willingham countered.

"Fine by us," Hessmann said.

Willingham dialed the cops.

As the Hardys and their friends waited, they compared notes about the challenges so far.

"One of the puzzles required us to retrieve pieces while the other put them together," Chet said.

"Guess who did which?" Daphne added.

Chet flexed his muscles. "Morton strong like bull, swift like eagle—"

"Brain-dead like roadkill!" Missy Gates chimed in from nearby.

"Are you and the redhead just in this to scout out the games and help the Hardy boys win?" Jay Stone added.

"Don't worry, Stone," Joe replied, "I'm sure *someone* will finish lower than you."

"We aced our first challenge, smart guy," Missy said. "We're moving on for sure."

"It takes more than one win to advance," Chet reminded them.

"We'll be counting our treasures when the game's done," Stone said.

"And *you'll* be counting bruises," Missy added. She and Stone laughed and headed across the warehouse.

"So much for friendly competition," Frank said.

About an hour and fifteen minutes after

Hessmann had first barged in, the police finally arrived to sort things out. Con Riley didn't look too pleased to be playing referee.

"We have an order barring them from filming in this warehouse," Hessmann argued.

"*I* have a court order on the way preventing enforcement of *their* order," Willingham said.

"But you can see our order right here," Scott said, waving the paper she and Hessmann had brought.

"My lawyer is bringing our paperwork over right now," Willingham countered.

Con Riley sighed and scratched his head. "You've got a writ, they've got a writ," he said. "I think this might be easier if I took all of you downtown and let a judge sort things out."

"That's fine by me," Hessmann said. He crossed his arms over his chest and scowled at Jackson.

"How is *that* fair?" Willingham asked angrily. "I've got a show to run here! This jerk doesn't have anything better to do than hassle me all day. It's fine if *he* goes, but I'm losing production time. Time *is* money—especially on TV."

"Can you prove to me this lawyer of yours is on the way, and that he's spoken to a judge about this order?" Riley asked Willingham.

"You bet I can." Willingham took out his cell phone and started punching numbers again.

Frank, Joe, Chet, and Daphne looked sympathetically at Riley as the legal struggle continued.

Catching their eye, the officer shrugged at them, then took the phone when Willingham handed it to him.

The officer spoke on the phone for a couple of minutes before handing the cell back to Willingham. Then he took a deep breath and said, "Okay, here's what I'm going to do. Mr. Willingham *does* have a court order on the way countermanding your court order, Mr. Hessmann. When that order gets here, I'll sort things out. Until then, Mr. Willingham can continue working on his show."

Willingham looked both relieved and happy.

"*However*," Riley continued, "he can't film in the section of the warehouse where the body was found."

"I can live with that," Willingham said.

"But that's in violation of our order!" Scott said.

Riley shrugged. "That's the best I'm going to do for you until his lawyer arrives. After that, you can all fight it out amongst yourselves."

"Could you wait outside?" Willingham asked Hessmann politely. "We've got a lot of work to do here."

"If I'm going outside, he should have to come too," Hessmann said, pointing angrily at Willingham.

"I'll go," Ms. Kendall volunteered. "I'll stay with him until our lawyers show up."

"Yeah, okay. Thanks," Willingham replied. "The crew and I will keep filming."

"Good enough," Con Riley said. He ushered Ms. Kendall, Mr. Hessmann, and his lawyer toward the door. As they reached it, the cop turned and said, "Mr. Willingham, I expect you to adhere to the highest safety standards until this gets settled. I'm holding you personally responsible. Understand?"

Willingham nodded and said, "Yes . . . Officer." But the words sounded forced.

As the cops and the disputing parties left the building, Willingham called out, "Okay, everyone. Back to work! I expect everything up and running again within fifteen minutes!"

"It's about time," Chet said.

The Hardys and the other contestants drifted back to the challenges they had been working on. Willingham checked with his technicians and then restarted each group of contestants in turn.

"So we'll be running our whole race again?" Frank asked.

"There's no need for that," Willingham replied. "The score was a tie when the two contestants reached the netting. We'll just pick it up from there."

"I thought this was a *reality* show," Joe said.

"*Simulated* reality," Willingham corrected. "The world's not really a postapocalyptic nightmare, you know." He grinned. "Besides, we're on a limited budget."

Joe and Frank looked at each other and shrugged. "TV . . . !" Joe said.

"Come on, let's go!" Bo Reid growled, doing some shadowboxing.

He and Joe re-entered the last part of the maze while Frank and Bo's redheaded partner stood on the sidelines and watched.

"When the Klaxon sounds, go!" Willingham said through a megaphone. Joe and Reid nodded their understanding and got ready.

When the siren went off, they both dashed onto the rope netting once again. They were more refreshed this time, and a bit more agile because of it. The boys reached the center of the netting simultaneously.

With a wicked grin, Reid hurled himself at the younger Hardy.

Joe ducked under Bo's lunge and tucked into a somersault. He rolled across the netting, came up near the edge, and quickly lowered himself to the floor. Joe sprinted across the finish line before Reid had recovered his footing.

"Yes!" Joe said, joining Frank and slapping him a high five.

"Great! Cut! Print!" Willingham yelled. He turned and headed for the next event.

"That wasn't fair!" Reid shouted as he clambered down from the net.

"All's fair in love and Warehouse Rumbles," Frank quipped.

"Catch you on the reruns, Bo!" Joe added.

"We'll see about that!" Reid said. He sprinted to catch up with Willingham, complaining loudly all the way. Reid's redheaded partner just shrugged and wandered off after them.

"What I admire most about Reid," Frank said, "is his good sportsmanship."

Joe laughed. He and Frank moved on to their next event.

A shallow pool, thirty feet across, had been set up in the area of the warehouse nearest the docks. In the middle of the pool stood a ten-foot-wide circular wooden platform. Three teams would be competing simultaneously in this game. The object was for the team member on dry land to use found objects to rescue the other team member from the center of the mock acid pool.

Joe, Lily, and a balding guy named Steve would be the people stranded in the middle of the fake acid. Frank, Todd, and Steve's partner, Kiff, would be working to get them out.

Ward Willingham stopped by to check the setup. He gave the nod to his crew, then moved on.

"Everyone ready?" the game's referee asked.

"Yeah," everyone said.

"Okay, when the Klaxon sounds, go! Three . . . two . . ."

But before he could say "One!" a loud creaking sound filled the set.

"Watch out!" someone yelled as a huge lighting tower toppled toward the pool.

6 Delayed and Dismayed

"Keep away from the water!" Joe called to the other contestants on the small platform in the middle of the pool.

The lighting tower seemed to fall in slow motion; the cables connected to it held back its descent. One by one, the lines snapped. Each sent a spray of sparks into the air.

"We'll be electrocuted!" Lily screamed.

"No," Joe said, "the wood platform should protect us. Just stay in the middle." He looked around, but saw no easy avenue of escape.

Chaos reigned on the outside of the pool. Technicians ran toward the tower, trying to stop its falling. Todd stood by the base, looking surprised and dazed.

"Someone kill the power!" Frank shouted. He

sprinted toward the stairs of a catwalk lined with auxiliary lights—it crossed twenty feet above the pool. As he ran up the stairs, Frank scanned the scaffold for anything that might help Joe and the others.

Below, snapped wires whipped around, hissing like electrified snakes. None of the technicians could get close enough to stop the tower's slow descent. The metal latticework of the tower groaned as it bent ever closer to the pool.

Frank raced along the overhead catwalk. "Jackpot!" he whispered as his brown eyes lit on a collapsible chain ladder lying on the grillwork deck. It was like a rope ladder, but instead it was made out of steel links and aluminum rungs. Frank recognized it as something that technicians often used to work above stages.

The elder Hardy snatched up the ladder and ran to the catwalk rail. "Grab this," he called down to Joe. "It's metal. Make sure it doesn't hit the water or anything when I drop it down to you."

"Check!" Joe called back up.

As quickly as he could, Frank fastened the chains to the catwalk rail and tossed the ladder to Joe.

The younger Hardy grabbed the ladder before it could hit the platform. He held it steady while Lily scrambled up.

The blazing electrical lights of the tower dangled only a few feet above the pool now; sparks still flew from the snapped cables. Somebody had pulled a fire alarm, and fire bells echoed through the old warehouse. Worried shouts from the staff and contestants rose above the noise. Ward Willingham's megaphone-amplified voice cut through the air. "What's going on?" he bellowed.

Frank didn't have time to answer. He helped the contestant named Steve onto the platform and then started to haul up the ladder as Joe began to climb. The next moment the light tower crashed into the water tank.

A huge *bang* shook the warehouse, and a shower of sparks, like a Fourth of July fireworks display, shot into the air. Joe lost his grip on the rickety chain ladder, but Frank grabbed him and pulled him to safety.

The pool below sizzled loudly for an instant as electricity arced through the water, and then the lights went out.

"I guess the circuit breakers blew," Joe said as the emergency lights clicked on.

"Not a moment too soon," Frank added. It wasn't quite dark yet, and dim illumination still filtered through the opaque windows near the top of the walls. The emergency lights, however, helped make the situation considerably less dangerous.

The Hardys, Lily, and Steve made their way down the stairway to the main floor. Even though the power wasn't on anymore, they were all careful to stay away from the wires that had snapped loose from the tower.

As they reached ground level, Ward Willingham dashed onto the set, his megaphone still clutched tightly in his hand. "What's going on here?" he demanded.

"The lighting tower collapsed," a technician said. "That guy was leaning on it when it happened." He pointed toward Todd, who was sitting across the room, holding his ankle.

"It wasn't my fault," Todd said. "Somebody pushed me into the tower."

Willingham frowned. Todd's sister looked upset too.

"Honest!" Todd said. "Look, my ankle's really messed up. Do you think I'd do that to myself?" He took his hand away from his leg to reveal a blood-stained sock.

"Are you badly hurt?" Willingham asked. "Do you need a doctor?"

"I'll be okay," Todd said.

Lily knelt down next to her brother. "I don't think he should compete anymore today," she said.

Willingham ran his hand through his hair in exasperation. "It'll take a while to clean up this mess, anyway," he said. Glancing at some of his crew, he added, "What are you waiting for? Get cleaning! We're on a schedule here!"

Making sure that the electricity was still off, the crew began hauling the broken lighting equipment out of the pool of water. As they did this two of the contestants competing in the event headed toward the warehouse door.

"Where are you going?" Willingham asked.

"Home," Steve said. "We're out of here before we end up as casualties on the evening news. Good luck, everyone." He and his partner left without looking back.

Willingham rolled his eyes and sighed, "Why me?"

"That's a very good question," Stacia said. She thrust her microphone into Willingham's face as her cameraman focused in on the producer. "Do you think the location you've chosen for *Warehouse Rumble* is inherently dangerous?"

"Where did you come from?" Willingham asked, clearly exasperated. "How did you get in here?"

"You've got lawyers, police, and soon, firefighters crawling all over—and you ask how I got here?" Stacia replied. "I repeat my question: Is this warehouse dangerous?"

"My client refuses to answer that!" interjected Willingham's lawyer as he and Herman Jackson ran up.

"My warehouse is *not* unsafe," Jackson added.

"Then why are you tearing it down?" the reporter countered.

"Get out of here, all of you!" Willingham said. "Jackson, have our lawyer get rid of this woman. I have a show to run."

"Not right now, you don't," said Riley as he

strode onto the set. The policeman looked as mad as a swarm of hornets. Hessmann and his lawyer followed right behind the cop.

"Mr. Willingham," Riley said, "you promised me that your show would run safely if I let you continue until your lawyer and Mr. Jackson arrived."

"Well," Jackson said, "now I *am* here—and I've got our writ—so the show can continue as scheduled."

"Not tonight, it can't!" Riley barked. "I've had it up to here with you lawyers and TV people. I'm taking *all* of you, and your court orders, down to the station until we can sort things out."

"That's fine with me," Clark Hessmann said. "I told you something like this would happen."

"Of course it's fine with him," Willingham countered. "That's what he wanted in the first place."

"Look," Riley said, "you've had a major accident here. The fire department is on the way. You're going to have to get their okay before I'll let you start shooting again."

By now everyone in the warehouse had gathered to see what the commotion was about. Chet and Daphne sneaked up next to Frank and Joe.

"Quite a show," Chet whispered.

"Let's hope it's not the final curtain—it was kind of fun," Frank replied.

Willingham sighed theatrically. "Okay, I guess we're shutting down for today." He turned to the contestants. "That's a wrap, everybody! See you all at nine tomorrow morning." To the crew, he added, "Get this fixed. Work overtime, if you have to."

"*After* the fire department finishes their safety check," Riley added. "Mr. Willingham, Mr. Hessmann, Ms. Allen, and the rest of you, come on. We've all got a date downtown."

"While we're there, I'd like to make a formal complaint against Mr. Hessmann," Jackson said. "I have a restraining order on him, and he's violating it right now."

Hessmann started to say something, but Riley cut him off. "One thing at a time," he said, clearly irritated. "Let's go."

Eyeing one another warily, Willingham, Jackson, Hessmann, Stacia Allen, and the lawyers all followed Riley out of the building. Willingham left Julie Kendall behind to supervise and coordinate with the fire department.

The Hardys and their friends headed for the parking lot. They got into the van just as the first fire truck arrived.

"Who'd have thought working on a reality show would be so exciting?" Joe said sardonically.

"Since there are TV dollars involved, I'm sure they'll sort it out by tomorrow morning," Frank said.

On the way home the brothers filled Chet and Daphne in on Joe's near-electrocution and Frank's timely rescue.

"So Todd Sabatine knocked down the lights," Chet said.

"He claimed he was pushed," Joe replied. "Frank, did you notice if Bo was around when the accident happened?"

Frank shook his head. "Nope. I was pretty busy saving your life." He smiled at his brother. "I don't remember seeing Reid in the crowd after the accident, though."

"That's a pretty extreme way to get revenge," Daphne said. "Even if Bo *is* a jerk."

"It's been a pretty extreme couple of days," Frank said.

"Don't tell me this is turning into another case," Chet moaned. "All I wanted was some fun, relaxation, and maybe a prize. Is that too much to ask?"

After several hours of discussion and banter, Willingham's lawyers prevailed. By the following morning the TV crew was ready to rumble once more. The mock toxic waste pool set was still a mess, though the staff hoped to have it ready for shooting again the following day. After checking the warehouse, fire marshals had given permission to continue shooting.

Despite their victory, the expressions on the faces of Willingham and his staff were grim as the four teens arrived at the set just before nine A.M. "We've had some trouble with the teams," Julie

Kendall told them. She forced a cheerful smile.

"What kind of trouble?" Frank asked.

"Well, after the . . . difficulties yesterday, some contestants decided to drop out. But don't worry, we've reconstituted some new teams from the remaining members. The competition will go on."

One of the renovated teams belonged to Bo. His redheaded partner didn't show up that morning. Bo was now paired with Lily, though neither of them seemed too pleased about it.

"With their partners out, they're lucky to be in the contest at all," Chet noted.

Todd, his ankle wrapped in an Ace bandage, was still hanging around the set to lend his sister moral support. The Hardys, Chet, and Daphne saw a few other gawkers hanging around, but no sign of Stacia Allen.

With the toxic-pool game out of commission, Frank and Joe were reassigned to another morning event. As luck would have it, they ended up paired with Chet and Daphne for a combined "tunnel run" through the bowels of the old warehouses.

"This is a test of cooperation, speed, and the ability to follow directions," Ward Willingham explained. "The world is in sorry shape in the future, and you'll be traversing treacherous tunnels in search of clues about where the final treasure is. Concentrate, and watch out for 'monsters' and other hazards." He smiled his patented Hollywood smile. "Your times through the course will be compared to those of the other teams. This will determine who advances into the next round of *Warehouse Rumble*. Got it?"

The Hardys and their friends nodded.

"All right, on the Klaxon, go!" Willingham said. The cameras rolled, and the four teens stood on the starting line. Joe held one set of directions to follow, and Daphne another. They were forbidden to exchange papers, and needed to work together toward their common goal.

With the blare of the siren, the two teams dashed off the line together. They leaped over several bits of "wreckage" and opened an old steel door. Beyond the door was a staircase leading down. Frank and Chet activated their lightsticks, and all four of them headed into the dark underbelly of the warehouse.

Once they reached the bottom landing they began reading off the directions they'd been given. A remote-control camera at the foot of the stairs tracked their actions as they raced into the darkness.

The tunnels had once supplied power and heating to the huge warehouses above. Long, heavy pipes and electrical conduits ran along the walls and ceiling. Many rooms—storage, maintenance, boiler rooms, furnaces, and water facilities—branched off the main tunnel. The whole structure formed a huge, dismal maze beneath the aging factory complex. Green-gray mold dappled the walls; dark puddles of rancid water dotted the floor.

The TV crew had placed huge fake spiders and other hairy mutant creatures in niches along the walls. Some of these hid cameras; most were only there for shock value. The first few gave the teens a start, but once they realized what the creatures were, they paid no attention to the rest. They couldn't be sure, though, if the rats prowling around were real, or merely another special effect.

They navigated skillfully through the tunnels, though the oppressive darkness made it difficult to tell how long they'd been in the maze.

"This way!" Frank called from up ahead. They were all tired and sweating, but knew they couldn't afford rest if they wanted a winning time.

"Right behind you!" Chet called. He and Daphne weren't as athletic as the brothers, and had fallen behind.

Suddenly, Daphne tripped and landed hard in a slimy puddle. "Oof!"

"Are you okay?" Chet asked. He offered her a hand up.

"Hang on," she said. A puzzled look drew over her face. "I think I found something."

She handed Chet her direction sheet while she groped around in the puddle for a second. She pulled her hand up again and held something next to the glowstick. The eerie light reflected off the object's surface.

In her fingers Daphne held a golden ring.

7 The Ring of Truth

"I think I found part of the treasure!" Daphne exclaimed.

Joe and Frank stopped and retraced their steps to where Daphne crouched, holding the ring.

"Where?" Joe asked.

"In this puddle," Daphne replied. She felt around for more, but didn't turn up anything.

"That's odd," Frank said.

"They told us pieces of treasure would be scattered through the courses," Chet noted.

"Maybe," Joe said, "or maybe it's just here to slow us down."

"Joe's right," Frank said. "This event is about time, not treasure."

"Yeah, okay," Daphne said. Chet helped her

to her feet, and they all began running again.

It took them nearly five more minutes to navigate the rest of the maze-like course. Even the dim daylight of the old warehouse seemed blinding as they dashed up the final stairs and across the finish line. The finish siren blared, and they stopped, panting, to catch their breaths.

Willingham came over and congratulated them. "You posted a great time."

"So that bit of treasure we found in the tunnel was just to slow us down," Frank said.

Willingham looked puzzled. He glanced at his staff. "Did you place some treasure for this game?" he asked. "That wasn't in the course design."

All of the crew nearby shrugged. "Not us, boss," said one.

Willingham scratched his head. "Show me what you found," he said.

Daphne held out her hand. In her palm rested a wide gold band, studded with emeralds.

Willingham took the ring and turned it over in his hand. "No treasure scheduled for the game looked like this. It's a really nice piece—if it's real." He peered over the edge of his omnipresent sunglasses, his eyes gleaming. "Let me ask Ms. Kendall and see if it belongs to any of the other contestants. Meet us in the refreshment area in a couple minutes. Okay?"

"Sure," Daphne said.

"You're the producer," Chet added.

Willingham grinned, handed the ring back to Daphne, and jogged off on his errand.

"Refreshments sound good," Joe said. "After that run, I could use a drink."

"All of us could," Frank said.

The four teens headed for the break area near the warehouse's main doors. As they arrived they spotted Stacia Allen and her cameraman poking around.

"I thought you'd been banned from the set," Frank said.

"Mr. Willingham and I reached an agreement," Ms. Allen replied. "I get to film any news events— just not the show itself."

"So you think there's going to be more news around the shoot?" Joe asked.

"Are you kidding? With the cops and the lawyers poking around, there's *bound* to be something juicy. Besides, you can't keep out the press, you know."

Frank and Joe glanced at each other and frowned. Neither thought much of Ms. Allen's press credentials. The four teens turned and headed toward a nearby cooler and pulled out some soft drinks. Ms. Allen and her cameraman followed.

"So," the reporter asked nonchalantly, "how is the game going for you?"

"Why not ask Mr. Willingham?" Joe replied.

Ms. Allen smiled. "So young, so brainwashed."

"We know which side our bread is buttered on," Chet said.

"I bet you do," Ms. Allen replied. She turned to Daphne. "What's that you've got in your hand?"

"Just a trinket from the game," Frank said.

"Can I see it?" Ms. Allen asked. Her cameraman edged closer to Daphne.

"Check with Mr. Willingham first," Daphne replied, clenching her fist tight.

"Speaking of whom . . . ," said Joe.

Willingham and Ms. Kendall had spotted the reporters and were hurrying toward the group.

"Ms. Allen," Julie Kendall said, "you *know* you're not supposed to interview contestants."

"I can if they're newsworthy," Ms. Allen replied coolly. "This group was involved in yesterday's accident."

"Not all of them," Willingham said. "Talk to these Hardy brothers if you want. Ms. Kendall and I need Soesbee and Morton for a moment."

"Fine by me, Ward," Stacia Allen said. She flashed an insincere smile.

Willingham shot the same smile back. "Be good, Stacia," he said. He and Ms. Kendall took Daphne and Chet into a corner a short distance away. Ms. Allen spoke to her cameraman briefly, then sat down on a folding chair next to the brothers.

She quizzed the Hardys for about ten minutes, trying to get them to implicate the creator and crew of *Warehouse Rumble* in the previous day's electrical accident. Frank and Joe didn't take the bait.

Allen's cameraman walked all around the trio as they spoke, filming from every angle.

Allen ended the interview abruptly. If she was frustrated by the Hardys' answers, however, she didn't let it show. She thanked the brothers and scurried off with her cameraman at the same time Chet and Daphne returned from their conference with Willingham and Ms. Kendall.

"So, did you give her any dirt?" Chet asked.

"Nothing she could even plant a dandelion in," Joe replied. They all laughed. "What did you turn up on the ring?"

"Ms. Kendall said it wasn't from the show's planned troves," Daphne said.

"It could still belong to one of the other contestants," Joe said.

"Or it could have been lost by someone who worked in the factory," Frank suggested. "We don't know how long it might have been there."

"I guess it could have been lost since before the factory shut down," Daphne agreed.

"I think Ms. Allen really wanted to get a look at it," Chet said.

"That woman," Joe said, "is having far too much fun with the show's problems."

"*Warehouse Rumble*'s troubles certainly have been a windfall for her, you have to admit," Daphne said.

"For Willingham, too," Frank added. "He may be complaining, but he's gotten a lot of news coverage."

"He asked me not to show the ring to anyone except the other contestants," Daphne said. "He's planning to use it as some kind of exclusive segment on the show."

"He said it lends 'authenticity' to the game," Chet added.

"Another good reason he could have planted it himself," Frank said.

"Forget all that," Joe said. "We need to concentrate getting into the next round of the game."

"Daphne and I already made it," Chet said. "Our scores on this last game pushed us through. You two are one contest behind because of the accident."

"Not for long," Joe said, smiling.

"I'll go see what our next assignment is," Frank said, jogging off to find Ms. Kendall.

The Hardys' next game turned out to be a puzzle made of junk parts. Their opponents in the game were Missy Gates and Jay Stone. The brothers had no trouble beating them to the finish. Missy and Jay scowled as Daphne came up and asked them about the ring. They spoke briefly, then the "Kings" duo sulked off.

"Was it theirs?" Frank asked.

Daphne shook her head. "I've checked with all the contestants. None of them lost any jewelry."

"It could still belong to someone who was disqualified yesterday, or who bugged out because of the trouble," Joe said.

"Maybe," Daphne agreed, "but Ms. Kendall said they didn't use the tunnels during shooting yesterday. She's checking with all the people who signed up, though. Since no one's claimed it, I'm going to wear it for luck." She pulled out a plain, golden piece of string from her purse, threaded the ring onto it, and tied the chain around her neck.

"Looks good," Chet said.

Bo Reid happened to walk by at that moment. "That's the only treasure you'll get in this game, losers," he said. He laughed and joined his new partner, Lily, in the refreshment area.

"It's more loot than *you'll* see!" Chet called after him.

The Hardys' morning win pushed them into the second round as well. Shooting on the next contests wouldn't begin until after lunch, so the teens piled into the van and headed downtown. It was nice to get away from the bickering and Hollywood politics for a while, and they all felt recharged when they returned to the warehouse at one in the afternoon.

As they entered, Ward Willingham came up to them. "Have you seen a prescription bottle lying around?" he asked.

All four teens shook their heads. "Who lost one?" Frank asked.

"Me," Willingham replied. "My sleeping pills. I thought they were in my coat pocket."

"Maybe you left them in your hotel room," Joe suggested.

"Maybe," Willingham replied. "I always have trouble sleeping when I'm on the road. I'm pretty sure I had them this morning." He sighed. "Dealing with that reporter woman is driving me nuts. I wouldn't be surprised if *she* took them, just to get my goat."

"That's a bit drastic," Frank said.

Willingham sighed ruefully. "All's fair in love and news," he said. "If you see the bottle, please return it to either me or Ms. Kendall."

"Check," said Chet.

"What's on the schedule for this afternoon?" Frank asked.

"We're doing some mutants and mayhem pieces," Willingham replied. "Scary monster–hunting stuff— to heat things up a bit. Ms. Kendall has your assignments." He nodded good-bye and headed for another part of the warehouse complex.

"If things heat up much more around here," Joe said as the producer left, "they'd be on fire."

"It's no wonder he has trouble sleeping," Daphne agreed.

The four friends got their shooting schedules for the rest of the day from Ms. Kendall. Chet and Daphne were slated for the first game of the afternoon: a clue-hunt that would take place in one of

71

the most remote and decrepit corners of the warehouse complex.

The two of them went and checked in with the production crew. Frank and Joe decided to tag along until their own event was ready to start.

The area chosen for the hunt was dark, though not as dark as the tunnels they'd run through earlier. The TV crew had piled up obstacles—mostly old machine parts—in a maze-like pattern. This way, the contestants could see sections of what lay ahead without seeing the whole picture.

"They're showing just enough to trick you about which way the maze is really going," Joe observed.

"Don't worry about us," Chet said. "I have the nose of a bloodhound."

"And the head of a fox," Daphne added, passing up the easy slam.

Chet looked at his watch. "Could one of you grab me a cola?" he asked. "I'm parched, but I don't want to miss the start of the event."

"Sure thing," Frank replied. "Want anything, Daphne? Joe?"

"I'll keep you company and grab something myself," Joe said.

"Nothing for me," Daphne replied. "I'm going to hit the rest room before the game starts. Here, Chet—you could use some good luck." She handed the ring on the string to Chet. He slipped it around his neck.

"See you in a couple of minutes," Frank said.

The brothers turned and picked their way through the set, heading for the refreshment area. Daphne disappeared behind some rubble toward the nearest rest room.

As the Hardys ducked under an old water tank, a strangled cry reached their ears.

"Ack, Help!"

8 That Was No Monster . . .

"That's Chet's voice!" Joe said.

They turned and ran back the way they'd come. The fake rubble slowed them down—it made moving in a straight line difficult. They could see what lay ahead of them, though, and what they saw gave them a shock.

Chet Morton was struggling with someone against one of the sets. But the thing he was fighting wasn't human. It had blue skin, bug eyes, and clawlike hands. The thing had Chet in a half nelson, and was trying to slip its other claw behind the big teen's neck.

Chet thrust himself backward, smashing his assailant into the wall. The insect-man grunted, and Chet slipped free of his grip. As he did, though, the mutant kicked Chet's legs out from under him. Chet landed hard on the floor, belly-flopping onto his face. The air rushed out of his lungs. The monster paused before reaching for Chet's neck.

"Hey, you!" Joe yelled as he and Frank charged forward.

The creature turned, slipped between two wide pillars, and disappeared into the darkness behind the set.

Joe ran after him as Frank stopped to help their friend.

"I'm okay," Chet gasped. "Just get that guy!"

Frank rose and pushed his way between the rusting pillars. On the other side he ran into Joe. "It's no use," Joe said. "The guy disappeared into this maze somewhere. I lost him."

"Rats!" said Frank.

He and Joe squeezed back between the pillars to Chet. Daphne had returned during the brief time they'd been gone, and was kneeling next to their friend. The big teen was sitting with his back up against the wall, taking a breather. "I'm fine," Chet said. "Did you bring that drink I asked for?" He smiled halfheartedly and coughed.

"Sorry. We didn't make it that far," Joe replied.

"Yeah—we got a little distracted," Frank added. He knelt down and patted Chet on the shoulder. "Next time, we'll keep our priorities straight."

Just then, Ward Willingham poked his head into

the start of the maze and said, "Everybody ready to rumble?"

"What, are you kidding?" Chet snapped.

"Having a monster try to grab one of the contestants before the start of the game is a really stupid stunt," Joe said angrily.

"Maybe it was 'cool' TV, but Chet could have been hurt," Frank agreed. "All of us would have been happier if he'd clobbered your monster."

"Mr. Willingham, I think you've taken the 'realism' of this game way too far," added Daphne.

"Whoa! Slow down," Willingham said. He stepped from behind the set into the starting area of the metal maze. "What are you talking about? What monster?"

The teens rose to confront the producer. "The monster that popped out of the set and attacked me," Chet replied. He pointed to reddish marks on his neck.

"He was wearing a blue-skinned, bug-eyed mutant costume," Frank said.

Willingham looked puzzled. "I didn't script any scare tactics before the start of the game," he said. "That might influence the competition. Plus, we don't have any bug-eyed monsters. They're a cliché. Ask Ms. Kendall if you don't believe me."

"You mean there's someone running around this warehouse in a monster costume who's *not* part of the game?" Joe asked incredulously.

"I hope not," Willingham said. "I'll notify security.

Mr. Morton, you take all the time you need to recover before starting your next challenge."

Chet nodded.

"Could your cameras have caught the attack on film?" Frank asked.

"I doubt it," Willingham replied. "The crew is just moving in from another set now. I'll check, though. Excuse me. I have to start another game. Morton can rest, but I'm still expecting you two boys on the set on time."

Frank and Joe nodded, fighting down the anger they still felt over this latest incident.

As Willingham walked away he punched the walkie-talkie function on his mobile phone and began checking with the rest of his crew.

"Could this all be part of some crazy publicity stunt?" Joe asked.

"Hard to tell," Frank replied. "If the story turns up on the evening news, we'll know. Chet, do you and Daphne need us?"

"We're fine," Daphne said.

"I'll be ready to go in a couple more minutes," Chet replied. "Then—mutants, watch out!"

Joe and Frank chuckled. "I want to poke around a bit," Frank said, "and see if we can figure out who was under that monster costume."

"Whoever attacked Chet was a pretty big guy," Joe said. "Bo Reid, Jay Stone, or even Willingham might have fit in those shoes."

"Jay's way too skinny," Chet said. "I could take him any day."

"Maybe not if he caught you from behind," Frank said.

"What about Todd?" Daphne asked.

"His ankle is busted up," said Chet.

"Maybe that's just what he wants us to think," Frank said. "Come on, Joe, lets see what we can find out before our game starts."

"Good idea," Joe replied. He and Frank ducked through the rusting maze set and headed back toward the center of the warehouse complex.

They passed through a number of the other game areas on their way back, but didn't see either Jay or Bo in any of them. They found Lily sitting on a darkened set, but neither Bo nor her brother was with her.

"Todd was here a minute ago. He just went to find Bo," Lily said. "Our next event is starting soon."

"How long has Bo been missing?" Joe asked.

"I haven't seen him since lunch," she replied.

"How's Todd's ankle?" Frank asked. "We haven't seen him this afternoon."

"He's been hanging out with me since lunch," Lily replied. "His ankle's getting better. Too late for the competition—unfortunately. The doctors said it's a minor sprain."

"Not enough to stop him from searching for Bo," Joe noted.

"One team member has to stay in the event staging area," Lily said. "Otherwise, we could forfeit."

"Speaking of forfeiting," Frank said, "we don't want to miss the start of our own event. See you later, Lily."

"Yeah," Joe added. "Good luck."

"You too," Lily said, waving as they left.

"Well," Joe said when they were out of earshot, "Todd may have an alibi, but Bo Reid's on the loose somewhere."

"That doesn't mean he attacked Chet," Frank said. "And we still don't know what Jay Stone's been up to."

A few minutes later they arrived at the staging area for their next event.

"About time you got here," Missy Gates said. She and Jay were leaning against a nearby wall, looking bored.

"So much for Jay's whereabouts," Frank whispered.

"You're our competition in this event?" Joe asked.

"Good work, Sherlock," Jay replied.

Before the banter could degenerate further, Ms. Kendall stepped in and explained the rules of the new game. She handed out several plastic gizmos that looked like flattened silver eggs attached to black elastic armbands. One end of each silver pod had a red crystal set into it.

"These are your wrist-laser blasters," she said. "You

can fire with the round button." She demonstrated, pressing a red button atop the silver sphere. "Your teams are on a monster hunt, trying to rid the area of mutants. Each enemy will have green target areas on their monster costumes. Hits in those areas will score points for your team."

"Where do we have to blast the Hardys to score points?" Stone asked.

Ms. Kendall frowned at him. "Shooting your opponents won't score any points at all. However, if a mutant hits your laser with its blaster, you'll *lose* points. If you drop below zero points, you're out of the event."

"Isn't it dangerous to flash lasers around?" Frank asked. "They can damage people's eyes."

"They're not real lasers," Ms. Kendall said. "It's just an infrared system—like the remote control on a TV. The studio special-effects department will add the laser effects later." She smiled and handed the blasters to all four teens. "Now, take your starting positions, and remember to keep to the marked trails. Monsters could be lurking around any corner. One Klaxon will sound to start the game, and another will end it. Ready to rumble?" Everyone nodded. "Good!"

She left as the two teams took their starting positions.

"Break a leg, Hardy," Jay said.

"Break both, Stone," Joe replied.

The siren sounded, and all four teens sprinted into the hunting area. Glowing greenish paint marked the areas that were out-of-bounds. As in most of the other games, the course was strewn with rusting machinery and other "postapocalyptic" props.

A mutant popped out from behind a rotting door. Joe blasted it with his wrist blaster. The monster howled and retreated.

"Pretty cool," the younger Hardy said.

Frank laughed and fired his fake laser as another creature appeared on a catwalk above them. The mutant shrieked and backed into the darkness once more.

After ten minutes the Hardys had tagged quite a few of Willingham's fake abominations. They'd taken a couple of hits themselves (their wrist lasers screeched each time they got blasted), but both brothers felt sure they had run up a good score.

Occasionally, they spotted Jay or Missy lurking around the ruins. Once, they saw Stone blasting in their direction. The Hardys resisted the urge to fire back.

"He's just wasting his time," Frank reminded Joe.

The mutants kept falling back, leading the brothers ever deeper into the game setting. The monsters' tactics were getting better as time wore on too. First they attacked only singly, then in twos, and now they appeared to be setting ambushes for the players to walk into.

Joe and Frank fought bravely onward. A screeching sound from the other side of a rusty wall told them that either Missy or Jay had been hit. Moments later a second screech indicated the other had been blasted as well.

"Sounds like they're in serious trouble," Joe said. Neither he nor Frank could resist smiling.

The brothers rounded a corner and saw Jay and Missy pinned down by five mutants. Frank and Joe waded in, blasting the monsters as they came.

"Get out of here! We don't need your help!" Missy shouted.

Suddenly a loud *bang* resounded through the warehouse. In the silence that followed, an eerie noise began to build. It was a scrabbling, screeching sound, like thousands of rusty door hinges.

Everyone, even the mutants, stopped and looked around, searching for the source of the clamor. A dented metal bulkhead lay thirty yards away—in the out-of-bounds area of the game. The portal yawned wide, opening into the dark maintenance tunnels beneath the warehouse.

As the contestants watched in horror, an endless swarm of rats burst from the basement.

9 Rat Rampage

A wave of dirty-furred rodents swept out of the underground and across the wooden floor. The rats' eyes gleamed red in the semidarkness of the warehouse. Their tiny voices squeaked and chittered, building into an awful cacophony.

Missy shrieked, but her cry was nearly drowned out by the noise from the pack.

"Everyone, outside! Quick!" Frank yelled.

The fake wreckage strewn through the warehouse hindered their progress as all four contestants, plus the mutants and Willingham's crew, scrambled to get out of the way of the ravenous horde.

The rats scampered forward like a hideous moving blanket covering the ground. The obstacles that blocked the humans' exit did little to impede the vermin's progress. The rats squeezed under rusting chicken wire and scrambled over corrugated pipes.

A cameraman stumbled and fell in the path of the rampaging swarm. Frank and Joe grabbed the man's arms and scooped him up. The rats nibbled at his shoes as the brothers dragged him to his feet.

As quickly as they could, they dodged through the set's obstacles and toward the nearest emergency exit.

The rats kept coming, though the swarm was less coherent now. The rats spread out, trying to find places to hide. The fake rubble set up by Willingham's crew presented plenty of concealment.

"They're almost as afraid of us as we are of them," Frank said, though no one but Joe and the cameraman heard him. The three of them kept running. The rats came right behind, nipping at their heels, threatening to overtake them.

Joe turned and toppled a big corrugated drainpipe into the path of the scurrying rodents. The rats squealed and scattered out of the way, buying the Hardys a few precious moments.

"Good work, Joe!" Frank said.

The cameraman stumbled again, but the brothers grabbed him under either arm and carried him out the emergency exit and into the parking lot.

Many people, both contestants and crew, were already outside. Stacia Allen stood across the unpaved street near her news van, filming the sudden exodus. Clark Hessmann was standing near Allen, and it appeared she might have been interviewing him before the commotion started.

"Allen and Hessmann are digging this," Joe said.

Frank nodded. "They both have something to gain from all this trouble."

The *Warehouse Rumble* cameraman thanked the brothers and joined the rest of the game crew. Moments later Chet and Daphne exited another area of the warehouse. They looked pale and shaken, but otherwise unhurt.

"Suddenly there were rats everywhere," Daphne said breathlessly, going over what had just happened.

"Our event was located in Rat Central Station," Joe replied.

"Ugh!" Chet said. "Where did they come from?"

"We heard a loud *bang*, and then they just started swarming up out of the underground," Frank said.

Ward Willingham emerged from the old warehouse looking angry and shaken. Stacia Allen and her crew rushed over to him. "What can you tell us about this latest setback to the trouble-plagued *Warehouse Rumble*?" Allen asked.

"There were rats in the warehouse," Willingham replied. "Is that *my* fault? We've had some bad luck, is all."

"You've had more than your share of misfortune," Ms. Allen said. "Some people are saying that all this trouble is an attempt to drum up publicity for show that hasn't been getting a lot of attention from your network."

Willingham's face reddened. He took off his sunglasses and glared at her. "Your show has been getting more publicity out of this than I have," he said angrily. "Maybe *you're* behind all our problems. Maybe *you* set those rats loose!"

Ms. Allen didn't back off. "So you admit there's been a lot of trouble?"

Clark Hessmann poked his head into camera range. "I told you there would be. I told you there were hidden dangers in these warehouses. Production should be closed down until a thorough—"

"That's enough!" Willingham said, cutting Hessmann off. He put one big hand over the lens of Allen's camera so that filming would be futile, then lit into the reporter and the activist. "You two can either back off or I'll have you ejected from this property. Hessmann, you shouldn't even be here to begin with."

"The restraining order only covers my proximity to Mr. Jackson. I'm well within my rights."

"And the unpaved road leading to the factory is public property," Ms. Allen added. "My van is parked on the road."

"Well, right now you're in *my* parking lot, and in

my face," Willingham growled. "So move it or lose it. Our truce is over. Get away from my production before I call the cops."

Reluctantly, Ms. Allen, her crew, and Hessmann retreated from the lot and returned to the WSDS van across the street. Once there, Allen began interviewing Hessmann again—though her camera often seemed to be pointed in the direction of Willingham and the crowd outside the factory.

"Bet she's got that zoom lens working," Chet ventured.

"Focused on Willingham, no doubt," Frank said.

Willingham wiped the sweat off his forehead and raised his hands to silence the crowd. "I'll talk to you all about this incident in a moment," he said. "Just hang in there with me. We're not licked yet. Not by a long shot." He turned to Ms. Kendall. "Get me an exterminator," he said. "I want the best. I want the set cleared out and ready to go tomorrow, no matter what the cost. The network will back me up."

"Yes, sir." Julie Kendall pulled out her cell phone and began dialing, then walked to a secluded area of the lot, away from the noise.

"All right," Willingham said to Hardys and the rest of the crowd, "this isn't the kind of wrap-up I'd planned for today's shooting. But, given the circumstances, I think we're done for the day."

A disappointed murmur ran through the crowd.

Willingham raised his hands once again for silence. "However," he said, "there is some *good* news to go along with the bad. First is that we got some great footage today. The competition is really shaping up, and *Warehouse Rumble* is going to be a *super* television show.

"Second, we've got a cast party tonight at Java John's in downtown Bayport. You're all invited, and I hope to see every one of you there. There will be food, refreshments, and music—all on the house, of course."

"Woo-hoo!" Jay shouted.

"Festivities begin at seven o'clock," Willingham said, putting on his best, though obviously forced, cheerful face. "Be there or be Rumblekill!" He pumped his fist in the air, and everyone applauded. "That's it. Head home and freshen up for tonight's blast. See you there!"

He turned and went to speak to Ms. Kendall, who had finished talking on the phone. Stacia Allen tried to snag a few folks for interviews as the crowd left, but all the contestants and staff gave her the cold shoulder. The Hardys, Chet, and Daphne ignored Allen too, and climbed into the Hardys' van.

The brothers and their friends went home, showered, and changed their clothes. Frank and Joe took some time to fill in their parents on recent events, then did the same for Callie and Iola (though Iola already knew much of the story from

88

Chet). The Hardys' girlfriends were too busy with their volunteer work to go to the party, though they wished the brothers continued luck in the game.

The four *Warehouse Rumble* contestants hooked up at Daphne's house at 6:45, then headed downtown together.

Java John's was a coffeehouse and eatery located on the first floor of a renovated building on Main Street, near the center of the city. Parking was usually plentiful in the area, but when the Hardys arrived, they found all the spots already taken. Many were occupied by vans from local TV and radio stations.

Joe pointed at one of the satellite trucks. "I guess we shouldn't be surprised that Willingham invited the press."

"I don't see Stacia Allen's WSDS truck, though," Frank noted.

"Maybe she's annoyed Willingham enough for one day," Chet suggested.

They found a parking spot two blocks away and walked back to the restaurant.

Java John's was fairly narrow but very deep. Mirrors along one sidewall gave the impression that the eatery was wider than it actually was. The front area had the coffee shop and a traditional soda fountain. The rear dining area had been roped off for the party.

A crowd of local reporters snapped the teens' pictures as the four friends moved to the back of the restaurant to join the festivities.

"I'll be signing autographs in the greenroom later," Chet said, pointing toward the kitchen to indicate where the media should meet him. The Hardys and Daphne laughed.

The food was good, and the fruit punch was just what they wanted after the long day. They mingled with the other contestants and members of the show's crew. Despite Chet's earlier joke, all four of them avoided talking to the media as much as possible.

Willingham's own people were covering the event as well, and the teens did a few interviews with them. "It's in your contract," the Hardys heard a staff cameraman remind Lily.

"I thought we were the only camera-shy folks here," Joe commented to Frank.

"I guess most people who didn't want publicity would skip this event altogether," Frank said. "I notice Lily's here, but I don't see her brother. I wonder if his ankle's acting up?"

"I see Missy Gates, too," Daphne said, "but not Jay Stone."

"I see Bo Reid," Chet said. "Unfortunately."

Reid was standing near the front of the party room, talking animatedly with a local reporter. After a while he gave up and headed for the refreshment tables, near where the four friends were standing. Reid spotted them and gave a sneering half-smile.

Chet waved at him.

"Don't press your luck," Joe whispered to him.

"It looks like Chet isn't the only one pressing his luck," Frank said. "Look."

Stacia Allen and her cameraman appeared at the front door of Java John's and headed toward the party. Ward Willingham moved to intercept her.

Allen and Willingham spoke heatedly for several minutes. Then Willingham stepped aside with a slight bow, and Allen and her cameraman swept in.

"Another victory for diplomacy at lens-point," Daphne said.

Willingham walked with Allen for a while, smiling obsequiously. Then—when he seemed certain that she wouldn't be trouble—he went back to mingle with the other members of the news media. The Hardys and their friends noticed, though, that Ms. Kendall was keeping a close eye on the reporters from WSDS.

"I could use a refill," Chet said, holding up his empty punch glass.

"Me too," agreed Frank.

All four of them headed toward the punch bowl. They ignored Ms. Allen, who was hovering around the food, cornering people with her microphone. Bo was her current target, though the Hardys and their friends had trouble feeling sorry for him.

As they refilled their glasses, Bo stormed out of the restaurant.

"Is applause appropriate?" Chet asked.

"Since we don't have tomatoes to throw," Daphne replied, taking a sip of her drink.

As Ms. Allen spotted the teens and began angling in their direction, the friends ducked back into the crowd. The restaurant had grown more crowded as the evening progressed. It was now quite hot, and almost unbearably noisy.

"I've had about enough of this," Frank said to the rest.

Joe nodded his agreement. "Let's thank Willingham for inviting us, and then head out."

"Wha—?" Daphne asked. She looked very bleary-eyed and disoriented.

"Are you all right?" Frank asked.

Daphne didn't respond, but Chet said, "I feel kind of woozy myself." He tottered back and leaned against the wall.

Joe looked at the half-empty punch glass in his hand and gasped. "There's something in the punch!"

10 Bad Medicine

Frank threw his glass to the floor. "Don't drink any more!" he said. "The hospital's not far away, but I doubt we should drive. I'll see if there's a cab out front." He staggered through the crowd toward the restaurant entrance.

The rest of the group dropped their glasses as well. Daphne and Chet leaned against each other, looking half-asleep.

Ms. Kendall came over and asked, "What's wrong?"

"Someone spiked the drinks," Joe replied groggily. "Keep everybody away from the punch bowl." He helped Chet and Daphne toward the door.

Stacia Allen tried to intercept them, but Joe pushed right past her.

"More *Warehouse Rumble* trouble?" she called after them as they staggered outside.

The world swam around Joe and his friends as they lumbered onto the sidewalk. Fortunately, Frank had a cab waiting. All four of them piled into the back.

"The emergency room," Frank said to the driver. "Step on it."

The cab pulled away from the curb and accelerated quickly down the street.

"What's . . . wrong with . . . us?" Chet asked.

Frank blinked slowly and tried to focus. "Remember Willingham's missing . . . sleeping pills?" he said.

"You think someone . . . put them in the punch?" Joe asked.

Frank looked at Daphne, dozing heavily on Chet's shoulder. "I'm willing to bet on it," he said.

They arrived at the hospital less than five minutes later and checked themselves into the emergency room. Frank explained what he thought had happened, and the hospital staff called Java John's to talk to Ward Willingham and discover exactly what was in the missing prescription. The doctors quickly figured out a remedy and administered it.

A short but uncomfortable emergency room stay later, the four teens were feeling well enough to be driven home by their parents. Fortunately, no one else at the party seemed to have been affected by the spiked punch.

Ironically, Chet, Daphne, and the Hardys did not sleep well that night.

At breakfast at the Hardys' home the next morning, all four teens felt angry and frustrated.

"You know," Chet said, "someone could have really gotten hurt from that stunt."

"Dad said the police are taking it very seriously," Frank said.

"There's talk they might even shut down the show," Joe added.

"It'd be a shame to spoil everything because of one or two bad apples," Daphne noted.

"The problems with *Warehouse Rumble* were all over the TV news this morning," Chet said. "UAN— the network producing the show—is even talking about pulling the plug."

"If this was some scheme concocted by Willingham to get publicity," Joe said, "it sure has backfired."

"There are plenty of other people who've bene-fited, though," Frank said. "Stacia Allen, for one."

"She was hanging around those refreshment tables," Chet recalled.

"Most of the party centered around those tables," Joe noted. "I don't think we can convict her just because of where she was standing." He yawned and stuffed another piece of French toast in his mouth. "I didn't see Clark Hessmann at the party, but he certainly wants to see the show stopped."

"The media attention—whether good or bad—might help Herman Jackson sell the warehouse area," Daphne suggested.

Frank took a long drink of milk. "I guess that Jackson wins if he can either sell it privately or get the city to buy it as a historical site."

"I'm betting one of the contestants put the sleeping pills in the punch," Chet said. "Having groggy opponents could make getting to the finals a cakewalk."

"Bo ducked out just before the trouble started," Daphne said. "Maybe he was just trying to nail us."

"There could be some motive that we don't know about too," Joe said. "It's hard to say, at this point."

"We'll just have to keep our eyes and ears open," Frank said.

"Or we could just drop out," Daphne suggested.

All four of them looked at one another and shook their heads. "Nah!"

After finishing breakfast they carpooled in the Hardys' van back to the warehouse. Many TV vans crowded the parking lot. One of Willingham's staff had been assigned to keep the reporters at bay and make sure the contestants and the staggering crew could get inside to work.

Willingham himself stood to the side near the old railroad tracks, speaking to a man dressed in overalls and a baseball cap. A logo on the man's uniform identified him as being from Pest-B-Gone Exterminating. A podium and some microphones had been set up nearby, but so far the press wasn't being allowed to speak with the producer himself.

"Eavesdropping, anyone?" Joe asked.

"Let's give it a shot," Frank replied. "It looks like they're keeping reporters away, not contestants."

He and the rest wandered close enough to catch Willingham's conversation.

"Darn foolish having one of your folks creeping around while my crew was working," the exterminator said. "My liability insurance won't cover that kind of stuff."

"I'm telling you," Willingham whispered back, "it *wasn't* one of my people. We were all at the party last night—footage from a half-dozen news shows can prove that."

The exterminator took off his hat and scratched his head. "Well, someone was lurking around the warehouse last night," he said. "I saw his flashlight. Couldn't find him when we looked, though."

"Maybe it was one of your own people," Willingham suggested.

"You think I don't know where my own crew members are?" the exterminator asked, offended.

"No, no, that's not what I'm saying," Willingham replied. "Look, you're sure the job is finished?"

"Finished as it can be overnight," said the exterminator. "You shouldn't set off any more fireworks in those tunnels, though. That smoke bomb is probably what stirred up the rats. I'd avoid any more pyrotechnics if I were you."

Willingham looked puzzled. "But, we weren't using any pyro in the tunnels."

Ms. Kendall came over and nudged the producer's elbow. "The vultures are restless," she said, glancing at the assembled media. "And we're pushing our shooting schedule as it is."

"Okay," Willingham said. "Let's get started."

He went to the podium and began speaking. Most of what he said the Hardys had heard before: bits about being proud of the show, about not having any more troubles than usual for a start-up TV program, and about how proud he was to be filming in Bayport.

He also denied rumors that his network, UAN, was close to pulling the plug on *Warehouse Rumble*. Though Stacia Allen's cameraman covered the briefing, she herself was conspicuously absent.

"Off digging up some more dirt, no doubt," Chet said.

"It wouldn't surprise me if *she* was the one sneaking around the warehouse with a flashlight last night," Daphne added.

"She's certainly unscrupulous enough," Frank said. "I'm wondering why she's not in the front lines here, though."

"Avoiding Willingham, maybe," Joe suggested. "How much more do you think he'll put up with before he gets a restraining order against her?"

"Not much, probably," Frank admitted.

About ten minutes into the "news conference," Ms. Kendall gathered the contestants and ushered them into the warehouse to begin preparations for shooting. If possible, the building looked even more ramshackle and run-down than it had the day before. The exterminators had clearly been pretty heavy-handed in rooting out the hidden rats. If she noticed the extra messiness of the sets, or the bitter tang in the air, Ms. Kendall didn't mention it.

"Even more postapocalyptic," Joe noted.

Chet and Daphne headed off for their new event while Frank and Joe met with Ms. Kendall about what they would be working on that morning.

The mutant hunt of the previous day had been declared a draw even though Frank and Joe had been well ahead on points at the time of the rat invasion. Ms. Kendall explained that the footage they had gotten of the rat swarm would make a great, unexpected end to that game segment.

"Gotta go with what makes good TV," Frank whispered to Joe.

"Even if it messes up our ranking," Joe replied. He sighed and shrugged.

"Don't sweat it," Frank said. "We'll ace whatever they throw us into."

Because of the change, the brothers would be facing Missy and Jay once again. This time the four would compete in a race across the catwalks that arced high above the warehouse floor.

"Due to the danger of the setting," Ms. Kendall said, "there will be no head-to-head confrontations in this race. If you meet an opponent on the course, you are both to stop and walk past each other. Any interference will result in the disqualification of the contestant responsible. Do you understand?"

The Hardys, Missy, and Jay all nodded that they did.

Staff members escorted the two groups to their starting points, and they all waited for the signal to begin.

With the sound of the siren the Hardys raced side-by-side up the metal stairway and onto the first catwalk. Illuminated arrows had been painted on the grating, so the brothers knew which way to go to the next checkpoint. At each station they had to retrieve part of a golden key that would help unlock the door that lead to the next challenge.

Despite the decrepitation of the warehouse, the metal catwalks had held up well over the years. As the brothers ran, they noted that some sections had been chained off and marked with large yellow "Radiation Warning" signs. Clearly the staff had checked over the skyway and had closed any area that they'd felt might be remotely hazardous.

The brothers claimed the first two parts of their

key quickly and without incident. As they approached the long bridge that spanned the two sections of the course, they spotted Jay at the far end. The bridge crossed the same area where the toxic pool event had happened two days before. The water-filled tank had been reassembled, and hidden machines made the dyed liquid bubble and look very dangerous. Clearly the producers had hoped that the contestants might meet in this very spot. The whole setup probably looked great on TV.

Stone and the Hardys dashed across the metal grating, each hoping to gain the advantage on the scaffold before the rules forced them to slow down and walk past one another.

They met closer to Jay's side of the bridge than the Hardys', and all three of them stopped dead still. Their eyes locked, and they stared one another down for a long moment.

"You can't block my progress," Jay sneered. "Those are the rules."

"You've got to step aside too," Frank said.

Reluctantly the three teens flattened themselves against opposite railings of the catwalk and edged forward. Just as they met, Missy appeared at the far end of the bridge. She was panting and out of breath, but dashed forward to catch up with the rest.

As she ran the whole bridge suddenly shook.

Missy fell onto the metal-grate walkway, and the

three boys had to grab the railings to stay on their feet.

"What's happening?" Missy cried, panic written across her face.

Frank's eyes darted to the link in the bridge behind her. The bolts holding the sections of the catwalk together had been shorn through. "Everybody hang on!" he called.

With a sudden lurch, the catwalk split in two.

11 Cat's Landing

The abrupt movement forced the teens to their knees. Each clung desperately to the catwalk's metal rail. The metal flooring behind Missy dropped away and, for a second, it looked as though she'd plunge to the warehouse floor twenty feet below.

At the last instant she grabbed hold of the nearest railing. The rail halted her descent, but she yelped in pain from the jerky stop. The bottom half of Missy's body hung precariously over the edge of the walkway. Her feet dangled in the open air. She tried to pull herself up, but didn't have the strength. Sweat beaded on her forehead.

"Don't let go!" Joe yelled.

"Like I would!" Missy hissed through gritted teeth.

"Grab on to my arm," Frank said, thrusting his

103

hand toward Jay, who had both arms wrapped around the catwalk railing.

"We can make a human chain," Joe said. "We can pull her up."

Reluctantly, Jay pried one arm loose and grabbed Frank's hand.

"Don't let go," Frank cautioned.

"Don't *you* let go," Jay shot back, his voice shaking.

Joe grabbed on to Frank's other hand, and the two of them edged toward Missy. They flattened themselves on the catwalk as much as they could, hoping that spreading out their weight might slow the bridge's collapse.

He stretched his hand as far as he could, but Joe still couldn't reach Missy.

"Don't let me die!" she cried.

"We won't," Joe said, trying to sound more sure of himself than he felt. He twisted around and extended his legs toward her. The extra length brought his feet well within her reach. "Grab hold and climb up!"

What remained of the bridge shook as Missy edged forward and grasped Joe's shoe and then his pant leg.

"Hurry up!" Jay called. He was sweating almost as much as Missy; his eyes darted around frantically. "This isn't gonna hold much longer!"

"I'm *trying!*" Missy shrieked back. She had climbed far enough now that Joe could reach down and grab her hand. He pulled her upward, and she scampered over the brothers and past Jay. As she did, she knocked the Hardys' cell phone from Frank's back pocket. It tumbled down, smashed on a metal strut, and splashed into the mock-toxic water.

"Let's go! Let's go!" Jay shouted as the brothers pulled themselves back up. He almost seemed ready to drop them, but Frank clung tightly to his hand.

As soon as Frank and Joe reached him, Jay turned, scrambled across the bridge, and headed down the nearby stairway. The catwalk shook as he went, swaying to either side. Frank and Joe nearly toppled off. Both got a good look at the bubbling green water in the pool below them.

"Anybody up for a high dive?" Joe asked.

"And join our cell phone?" Frank replied. "No thanks."

The bridge creaked, shuddered, and lurched down another few feet, making the angle of their climb even steeper. A camerawoman suddenly appeared at the far end of the span and tossed a rope down to them.

Frank and Joe grabbed it and quickly ascended. "Thanks," they both said as they left the bridge behind.

"We're not down yet," the woman replied. She turned and descended the stairs as quickly as possible, the brothers close on her heels. As they all reached the ground floor, the bridge gave a final groan, and the part the Hardys had been climbing on only moments before crashed into the pool. Yellow-green water sprayed high into the air.

"Is anyone hurt?" Ms. Kendall called as she dashed onto the set.

"Something's wrong with my arm," Missy said. Tears streamed down her face, and she looked like she was in considerable pain.

Ms. Kendall motioned to a paramedic who had followed her into the room. Apparently, after the recent trouble, the production now felt it wise to have medical personnel on the set at all times.

"She probably shouldn't stay in the game," the medic said after examining Missy for a few minutes.

"We ought to sue you!" Jay said.

"We'll see she's taken care of," Ms. Kendall replied. Seeing that this didn't calm Jay any, she added, "And we'll make sure you can continue in the game if you want to."

"You bet I'll continue!" Jay said. He glared at Joe and Frank. "You Hardys attract trouble like a magnet." He and the medic took Missy away from the game set so she could get further treatment.

"Don't say thanks for saving her life," Joe muttered.

Ms. Kendall looked up at the damaged section of catwalk. It angled down into the pool like an immense, metal-mesh slide. She frowned. "I don't get it," she said. "We ran the same exact event across that same section of bridge yesterday. There were no indications of any problems then."

"Maybe the connecting bolts wore out over the course of the game," Joe suggested.

"Metal fatigue makes sense," Frank said. "This whole place is pretty rusty." Something in the elder Hardy's brown eyes told Joe that Frank didn't believe the theory he was espousing.

Joe nodded, though. "Yeah. Metal fatigue." They could discuss the other possibilities later.

Just then, Ward Willingham burst onto the set. "Not *more* trouble!" he moaned.

Ms. Kendall didn't say anything. She just pointed to the broken catwalk.

Willingham took off his dark glasses and slapped his head. "Two broken game sets?" he said. "How long will it take to clean this up?"

"I don't know if we *can* clean . . . ," Ms. Kendall began—but when she saw Stacia Allen and her cameraman lurking nearby, she suddenly stopped talking.

Willingham followed Ms. Kendall's gaze and spotted Ms. Allen as well. He stormed in her direction, shaking his fist. "You've got a lot of gall prowling around here after the stunt you pulled on your broadcast last night."

Ms. Allen tried to look innocent but didn't do a very good job. "I don't know what you mean," she said. "I've been abiding by our agreement."

"Maybe by the words," Willingham growled, "but not the spirit. I didn't authorize you to film that ring. And I certainly didn't authorize you running pictures of it on your show."

"That ring wasn't part of the game prizes," Ms. Allen replied. "It was news. So I was within my rights to run a story about it."

"Are they talking about the ring Daphne found?" Joe whispered to Frank. Frank shrugged.

"How did you know it wasn't part of the game treasure?" Willingham asked. "You never asked any of my people about it."

"I have my sources," Ms. Allen said smugly.

"You *knew* I was saving that discovery for a surprise in my own broadcast," Willingham said. "I want you out of here, now!"

"Maybe my lawyers should call your lawyers," Ms. Allen replied.

Julie Kendall stepped in front of the Hardys, blocking their view of the ongoing argument. "Well," she said, "I certainly don't think you boys need to hang around here just to listen to Ms. Allen and Mr. Willingham. Why don't you head to the refreshment area? I'll make sure someone comes and talks to you about your next event."

The brothers left. When they got to the break area they found Chet and Daphne already there.

"Waiting for your next event?" Frank asked.

"Nah," Chet replied. "We aced ours. We're on to our next round. How about you guys?"

"Cancelled again," Joe said, "on account of

sabotage." He and Frank quickly explained what had happened, and the argument between Willingham and Stacia Allen that had ensued.

"Where did that news vulture get pictures of my ring?" Daphne asked, clearly annoyed.

Chet shrugged. "She's had plenty of opportunities since you found it. And she's pretty clever."

"That and a good zoom lens will get you almost anything," Joe added.

"Anything except scruples," Frank noted. "I suppose it's possible her crew might have planted the ring in the first place, just to stir things up."

"Or maybe it was lost by whoever's causing all this trouble on the set," Joe suggested. "I don't believe that metal fatigue caused that catwalk to break any more than you do."

"Sabotage seems more likely," Frank admitted. "I'm sure the crew checked the whole walkway for safety before they started running events on it. It's unlikely they'd miss something that would cause the bridge to collapse."

"Well, the problem didn't cause much of a stir in the rest of the sets," Daphne said. "We didn't even hear about it."

"The show must go on," said Chet.

"Not for us, it won't," Frank said. "Not unless we actually get to finish some of our contests."

"They can't cut you from the rumble because of bad luck," Daphne said. "That wouldn't be fair."

"Hey, we're talking about *television* here," Joe said. "Fair doesn't enter into it."

"I'm sure they're getting some great footage out of your events," Chet said.

Joe arched one eyebrow. "Maybe good enough footage to inspire sabotage?"

"Could be," Frank replied. "That's a mighty risky strategy, though. Getting caught would be a sure way to get sued."

A few minutes later Ms. Kendall showed up and took the Hardys to another alternate event. It was a relay race across the broken pylons on one of the old docks behind the warehouse. The Hardys darted easily across the concrete platforms; their competitors, though, ended up falling into the bay. After helping fish out the losers, the brothers headed for lunch in the break area.

In order to keep film rolling, Willingham had brought in catered food. This allowed him to pick up the pace on events and make up for lost time. Chet and Daphne must have eaten already and moved on to their next event, because the Hardys didn't see their friends in the area.

The mood of the contestants who *were* having lunch, though, was tense. Many fidgeted nervously as they ate. The Hardys spotted Jay and Missy standing at the back of the line that wound toward the food table. Missy's heavily bandaged left arm was in a sling. The two of them scowled at the brothers as the Hardys joined the end of the line.

Just as they lined up, someone bumped into Joe from behind. "Hey! Watch it!" said a gruff voice.

Joe spun and found himself nose-to-nose with Todd Sabatine. The big teen's ankle was still wrapped in an Ace bandage, and he was using a cane to help himself get around. Lily came to her brother's side as Todd glared at Joe.

"Sorry," Joe said. "I didn't see you."

"You should be more careful," Lily chided. "My brother's not very mobile." Her new partner, Bo, kept an eye on all of them from a table nearby.

"I said I was sorry," Joe repeated, fighting down a twinge of anger.

Jay, who was directly in front of Joe, nudged the younger Hardy. "Yeah, Hardy," Jay said, "watch it!"

Joe was about to say something when Jay suddenly pointed at the floor. "What's that?!" he asked in a very loud voice.

Everyone in the area turned and looked. On the floor, near Todd's feet, was an orange prescription bottle.

Joe stooped down, picked it up, and read the label. "It's Mr. Willingham's missing sleeping pills," he announced. He held the bottle out toward the Sabatines. "Do you know anything about this?"

"You're not going to pin this on us!" Todd said. "*You* probably planted it there!"

Without warning, Todd lunged at Joe.

111

12 Tossed Out

Todd's sudden tackle caught the Hardys completely off guard. Before Frank could react, Joe and Todd crashed to the floor.

The two of them rolled around on the old wooden planking for a few moments, each trying to get the advantage on the other. Joe had quite a bit of wrestling experience, but Todd was bigger and heavier than the younger Hardy. As Todd attempted to put Joe into an armlock, Frank grabbed Todd's shirt and tried to pull him away.

Most of the other people in the area stood and watched, a mixture of surprise and anxiety on their faces. Missy and Jay cheered the fight on.

Several members of the staff stepped in to help

112

just as Frank wrestled Todd off of Joe. Working together, they managed to separate the two teens.

"What in the world is going on here?" boomed Ward Willingham.

"We found your prescription, Mr. Willingham," Joe said angrily, "lying on the floor next to him!" He pointed accusingly at Todd.

"It's a setup!" Todd shot back. "Those two have been near the scene of every accident on this set. *They're* the ones behind all this trouble!"

"That's a lie," Frank said.

"Now look," Willingham said, raising his voice even more, "things have been tense on the set and we've had some problems, but anyone who wants to stay in the competition *must* stay focused." As he turned toward Todd he found Stacia Allen and her cameraman in the way. He scowled and stepped around them.

"Mr. Sabatine, I'm sympathetic to your wanting to cheer your sister on," Willingham said. "However, I think it's best if we close the competition to spectators at this point."

"But that's not fair!" Lily protested.

"I'm sorry, but that's my decision." Willingham looked at Missy. "Sorry, Ms. Gates. The policy applies to you, too."

Missy stopped picking her teeth with her one good hand and sneered at him. "Typical," she said. She stood and headed for the door.

Jay went with her. "You haven't heard the last of this," he called. "I'll be back!"

Willingham let out a long sigh and rubbed his forehead.

Stacia Allen stepped up and thrust her microphone in his face. "How does this latest setback make you feel?" she asked.

"It makes me feel," Willingham said slowly, "like I've had more than enough of your intrusions." He signaled to a couple of security guards standing nearby. "Take Ms. Allen and her crew out of here."

The guards stepped forward and began escorting the WSDS team from the building. "You can't throw me out!" Ms. Allen called back over her shoulder. "We have free press in this country! We—" The slam of the warehouse door cut off the rest of her words.

Willingham smiled slightly. "Right now," he said wryly, "we have freedom *from* the press. At least on *my* set." He turned back to the rest of the assembled cast and crew.

"Now, if we can avoid any more outbreaks of . . . enthusiasm," he said, glancing warningly at the Hardys, "maybe we can get back to work. Please finish up your lunches and then move on to your next assignments. I want to thank you again for sticking with us through all of the tough spots." He turned and went off to discuss something with Ms. Kendall.

Lily glared at the Hardys, then escorted her

brother to the door. Willingham's security guards kept their distance but watched carefully as Todd left. Missy followed him out.

"Do you think Todd dropped those pills?" Frank asked.

"He was right next to them," Joe said. "But Jay was pretty close too. Maybe they fell out of Todd's pocket, or maybe Jay planted them, or maybe someone was trying to use sleeping pills to knock out the competition again."

"Todd's not in the game, though," Frank said. "So if someone dropped those pills on purpose, the target had to be either Jay, Bo—he was pretty close by too—or us."

"We don't have a lot of friends on this set," Joe admitted, "aside from Daphne and Chet. Taking us out would make things easier for some of the other players."

Frank nodded. "And there *have* been a lot of accidents during events we've been at. Even Todd noticed that."

"Let's not get too paranoid," Joe said. "Scuttling this whole show seems a better motive for the trouble than removing a few contestants."

"That depends on the prize, I suppose," Frank responded. "Of course, only Willingham and his staff know what the final treasure is. All we've seen so far is some golden keys."

"Yeah," said Joe. "And we know that Daphne's ring

wasn't a part of whatever Willingham has stashed."

"So Todd, Bo, or Jay could have been setting us up, or any one of them could have been setting up any one of the others," Frank concluded.

"Or it could be someone we're not even considering," Joe added. "In any case, I doubt that the prescription has just been lying on the floor for the last day, waiting for someone to find it."

Frank laughed. "Yeah. I think we can rule that out."

The competitions continued after lunch. The number of contestants in *Warehouse Rumble* was shrinking, due to elimination during the game and some contestants choosing to drop out because of the continuing accidents. As semifinals drew near, the competition became even more fierce.

The new alliance of Lily and Bo only grew stronger. Amazingly, Jay—playing solo—squeaked through his afternoon challenge. Chet and Daphne also survived—though barely.

"Chet fell in the water, but I managed to cross the finish line before anyone from the other team did," Daphne confided to Frank and Joe.

Chet smiled sheepishly and toweled the water from his hair. "Hey, I said I had catlike reflexes—not catlike balance."

The Hardys' afternoon challenge involved retrieving clues from a course using remote-control cars and then using them to solve a puzzle. The bodies of the cars had been modified so that each resembled a giant insect. The effect was fairly comical, though the brothers admitted that it might look good on TV.

"If this show doesn't become a hit as is, maybe they can spin it off as *Battle Bugs* or something," Joe joked between rounds as technicians serviced the bug-cars.

"*The mutant mania of the future that everyone with three eyes is talking about,*'" suggested Chet. He and Daphne had come to watch the Hardys' event, since their own had already finished. "*Go buggy or bug off!*'"

"You could have been an ad writer, Chet," Frank said.

"I may be," Chet replied. "After Daphne and I win this competition, of course."

"Of course," Daphne said with a smile.

"Unless we beat you to it," Joe said.

"Of course," added Frank.

Once the technicians had finished preparing the remote-controlled mutants, he and Joe returned to the contest. They managed to squeak out a win, though their opponents nearly completed the puzzle first. Fortunately the Hardys' competitors misread a critical clue, and the brothers surged ahead of them at the last minute.

As Frank, Joe, and their friends headed to check on their next challenges, they heard one of the technicians say, "Great TV."

"Yeah," Chet said. "You guys did good."

Frank nodded wearily. "I'm beginning to feel it, though."

"With the obstacles we've had," Joe said, "I feel like we've done *twice* the number of games as everyone else." He wiped the sweat from his forehead with the back of his arm.

"Look at these two," Daphne said. "You'd think they'd just run a mile."

"Five miles," Chet said.

"Brain work can work up a sweat too," Frank said.

"Time to refuel, I think," said Joe.

Within a few minutes they'd reached the refreshment area. The brothers felt relieved that most of the other contestants looked just as bushed as they did. Lily and Bo seemed equally tired. Jay looked utterly exhausted.

"Too worn out to hassle us, I hope," Joe said.

As the four friends sat down in folding chairs on one side of the break area, the warehouse doors suddenly opened and Con Riley walked in. He was followed by a small contingent of police officers, and a slender older woman with silver hair twisted up into a bun.

"Where is it?" the woman whispered harshly to Riley. "Do you know who has it?"

"Take it easy, Ms. Forbeck," Con Riley replied. "We have protocols to follow."

In the wake of the police came Stacia Allen and her cameraman, camera rolling and microphone ready.

Spotting the reporters, Ward Willingham moved to cut them off. "What's going on here?" he asked. "Ms. Allen is no longer welcome on my set. Officer, would you please ask her to leave?" The producer was clearly struggling to keep his temper under control.

"Good afternoon, Mr. Willingham," Con Riley said. "I'm afraid we'll have to discuss the status of Ms. Allen later. I have a warrant to search these premises." He held out a piece of paper so the producer could examine it.

Willingham glared at Allen and her cameraman. "Another one of your stunts, I suppose," he said.

Stacia Allen shook her head. "Nope. But I'm loving every minute of it. I told you you can't kick out the press." She directed her cameraman to focus on Willingham as he took the piece of paper from Officer Riley.

Con Riley scanned the crowd until his eyes lit upon the Hardys and their friends. He walked over to them, looking very stiff and formal.

"Hi, Con. What's up?" Joe asked.

"Don't tell me that Reid character swore out a complaint against us," Frank said.

"No, Frank," Riley said. "In fact, I'm not here to see you and your brother at all." He turned toward Daphne and Chet. "Ms. Soesbee," he said, "I'm afraid I have to ask you to come downtown."

13 The Lady of the Ring

Chet rose and stood between Daphne and Officer Riley. "What's all this about?" he asked angrily.

Frank and Joe joined their friend. "Are you arresting Daphne?" Joe asked.

"I'd rather not," Riley replied, "but I will if that's what it takes."

The older woman came forward and looked at Daphne with hawklike green eyes. "Is she the one?" Ms. Forbeck asked. "Is she the one who stole my ring?"

"What are you talking about?" Daphne asked. She looked both puzzled and scared.

Ms. Forbeck thrust a bony finger at Daphne. "There it is!" she said, pointing to the ring on the string around Daphne's throat. "She *is* the one. Thief! Thief!"

"Take it easy, Ms. Forbeck," Con Riley said.

"Who is this old bird?" Chet asked.

"Be polite, Morton," the policeman snapped. "This is Carla Forbeck, one of Bayport's most prominent citizens."

"And that ring was among the jewelry stolen from me fifteen years ago!" Ms. Forbeck said indignantly.

"Well, *I* didn't take it," Daphne said. "I was in preschool fifteen years ago. I just found this the other day."

"That's what we want to talk to you about downtown," Riley said.

"Couldn't you question her here?" Frank asked. "She's competing on this show."

"That's okay, Frank," Daphne said. "I think Chet and I are done for the day, anyway."

"Well, if you're going downtown, I'm going too," Chet said.

"And us," added Joe.

"Won't that hurt your standing in the game?" Daphne asked, worry written across her pretty face.

"What's more important: a TV show, or a friend?" Frank said.

Nearby, Ward Willingham frowned. "Well, if you're going to haul off my contestants, do so," he said. "And take those news snakes with you. They're not welcome on my set."

Stacia Allen smirked at him. "I think we have what we need," she said. "The real story now is going to be told at the police station."

"You'll have to talk to Chief Collig about that," Riley said. "Okay, all of you, let's head for the squad cars."

Daphne, the Hardys, and Chet followed the police toward the door. Stacia Allen and her cameraman followed. The brothers tried not to notice Jay Stone laughing while they left.

"Don't worry," said Ms. Kendall, who was standing at the doorway. "We've nearly finished shooting for the day. I'll try to make sure you're not left out."

The four friends nodded their thanks to her.

It took only a few minutes to reach police headquarters downtown. As the cops figured out which interview rooms they were going to use, the brothers put in a call to Daphne's mom. The Book Bank—the store the Soesbees owned—was only a few blocks away, and Kathryn Soesbee arrived at the station in no time. The police had decided to let her accompany her daughter during the questioning. Since the Hardys and Chet were involved with the discovery of the ring, they were allowed to sit in as well.

Con Riley ushered all of them into a small meeting room near the rear of the station. An oval table surrounded by chairs was in the center of the room.

Ms. Forbeck and her lawyer took their seats, as did a police stenographer.

As the rest seated themselves Kathryn Soesbee asked, "Would someone please tell me what's going on here?"

Con Riley turned to the older woman. "Ms. Forbeck," he said, "maybe you should start."

The slender, silver-haired woman stood. "My name is Carla Forbeck," she said. "Possibly you have heard of me. My family is prominent in Bayport society, and has been for a hundred and fifty years.

"Fifteen years ago, on the night of April sixteenth, my ancestral home was broken into and robbed. Many valuable pieces of jewelry were taken. The thief was never caught, and none of the goods have ever resurfaced—until now." Her cold green eyes fell on the ring dangling around Daphne's neck. "I saw the ring this morning on the WSDS News broadcast."

Daphne put her hand to her throat. "So you're saying this ring is part of the jewelry that was stolen from you?"

"I would recognize it anywhere," Ms. Forbeck said. "But, in case you require proof, my lawyer has brought photos from the insurance claim." Her lawyer reached into his briefcase and laid a photo on the table.

Daphne, the Hardys, Chet, and Ms. Soesbee looked at it.

"That's the same ring, all right," Joe said.

Daphne took the ring off of the string and handed it to Carla Forbeck. "Here, Ms. Forbeck," she said. "I was only keeping it until the owner turned up."

"Where did you find it, Daphne?" Con Riley asked.

"In the basement of the old warehouse," Daphne said.

"The show had a contest that involved going into the tunnels beneath the complex," Frank explained. "We were running a race when Daphne stumbled. She found the ring in a puddle on the floor."

"At first we thought it was one of the game's prizes," Chet said, "or something lost by one of the other contestants or crew."

"When that turned out not to be the case," Joe said, "we theorized it might have been lost by someone who had worked in the warehouse before it closed."

Daphne nodded. "We didn't think the owner would turn up, so I decided to wear the ring as a good-luck charm."

Con Riley looked at Ms. Forbeck. "It's lucky for you that she did. Otherwise, you might never have found it."

"That's true," Ms. Forbeck said. "And now that I've heard her story, I don't believe that she had anything to do with the theft. She would have been little more than a baby when my jewelry disappeared. I will, of course, be dropping the charges."

Kathryn Soesbee let out a long sigh of relief. "Well, thank goodness!" she said. "Can I take my daughter home now?"

"I don't see why not," Con Riley replied. "We'll just want a signed statement from her before she goes. And from the rest of you as well," he added, looking at the Hardys and Chet.

"No problem," Joe said.

Filling out the paperwork took about an hour. As the four teens and Daphne's mom were about to leave, Ms. Forbeck stopped them near the station door. "I want to thank you for finding my ring," she said. "Though I wonder how it came to be in the warehouse in the first place."

"That complex is huge," Frank said. "I'm sure a lot of people have come and gone from it over the years."

"In its heyday there were probably hundreds of workers in there," Joe added. "Maybe thousands."

"Yes," Ms. Forbeck replied. "You're probably right. Well, if I'm lucky, maybe the rest of the jewels will turn up one day. That nice policeman said they'd send someone over to check the area where you found the ring. After so much time, though, I doubt they'll turn up many clues."

"You never know," Frank said.

"Good luck," Daphne said.

They said their good-byes to Ms. Forbeck, then headed to their respective homes. All four teens were so exhausted by the day's ordeals that they quickly fell into deep slumbers.

The news that greeted the teens the next morning was good. Despite their absence at the end of the previous day, Ms. Kendall called to say that both the Hardys and Chet and Daphne's team had made it through to the next round of the contest. Jay Stone and the Sabatine-Reid team had advanced to the semifinals as well. Missy apparently felt well enough to compete alongside Jay. Her left arm was still bandaged, but she wasn't using the sling anymore. Though the Hardys and their friends weren't scheduled to go head-to-head right away, it was clear they might soon have to face one another.

"May the best team win," Chet said, as they congratulated one another over breakfast at the Morton house.

"Break a leg, both of you," Joe said, smiling.

"This sure is a strange case," Frank said. "We've got accidents, a dead man in a chimney, a game with treasure at the end, purloined prescriptions, stolen jewels, monster-masked intruders, and mysterious lights in the warehouses at night. . . ."

"And rats," Daphne added. "Don't forget the rats."

Frank sighed. "If we weren't running ourselves ragged, maybe we'd see how it all fits together."

The four of them finished breakfast and headed back to the old warehouse. As they pulled into the parking lot they spotted Stacia Allen's news van parked, as usual, across the street.

"If there's trouble, she's here on the double," Joe said.

"With luck, she'll stay on *her* side of the street today," Chet said.

On their way inside they met Officer Gus Sullivan coming out of the warehouse. He was covered in dirt and looked very unhappy.

"Anything wrong?" Frank asked.

"Just wasted the morning searching the area where your friend found that ring," Sullivan said, brushing the grime from his uniform. "Didn't find anything but muck, and rat tracks. Call us if you kids turn up anything. And, if you do, be sure you ask for Officer *Riley*." He gave a half-smile, indicating that he hoped Riley might have to dig through the basement next time.

The four teens chuckled. "We'll keep in touch," Joe said.

They checked with Ms. Kendall for their assignments, and discovered—somewhat to their relief—that the four of them would not be facing one another that morning.

"That increases the chances of one of our teams getting to the finals," Chet said enthusiastically.

They split up, and the Hardys headed for the same side of the warehouse where they'd encountered the rat swarm.

"I hope those exterminators did their job," Joe said.

Their challenge consisted of clue reading and navigating another maze. They and their opponents, Lily and Bo, would start from opposite ends of the course. The first team to reach the middle and sound the Klaxon would win and advance to the finals.

The brothers waited for the siren and then raced forward into the maze.

The labyrinth had been constructed out of both old warehouse rooms and new obstacles put in place by the *Warehouse Rumble* staff. Windows and other light sources had deliberately been blocked off to make navigating and reading the clues more difficult.

Rusting metal machines and crumbling plaster walls pressed in around them. The atmosphere was heavy and smelled of mold and decay. They tired quickly and their breath came in labored gasps.

"You know," Joe said, pausing for a second, "I'm starting to wonder why we signed up for all this abuse."

"Let's just keep going," Frank said. "We're almost to the finals." He and his brother began running again.

An eerie, mournful wail stopped them in their tracks. "He-e-elp!"

The Hardys couldn't see who was yelling, but the cry came from the out-of-bounds area, beyond the course. Joe and Frank looked at each other, wondering—for a moment—whether they should risk leaving the game.

"It could be part of the contest," Joe said. "A trick."

The cry came again, more desperate this time. "Help!"

Without further hesitation, the two of them leaped a rusting barrier and raced forward.

"Where are you?" Frank called. "Shout again so we can find you!"

No reply came, but Joe spotted a bulkhead in the floor ahead of them. "Maybe someone got trapped down there," he said.

The brothers ran across the worm-eaten planking toward the bulkhead. They were moving so fast and concentrating so hard on listening for another cry for help that neither one of them noticed the rotting floorboards creaking under their weight.

Suddenly the floor gave way, and the Hardys plunged down into darkness.

14 Deep Down Darkness

"Frank? Are you all right?"

"Yeah, I think so. How about you?"

"I think so. I can't see anything."

"Me neither."

"Good," Joe said. "I was worried that I might be blind."

"We must have slid into the basement of the warehouse," Frank said. "Hang on. I have a flashlight in my pocket."

"Isn't that against the rules?"

"I don't think we're on the clock right now." Frank pulled a small penlight out and shone it around.

The area looked a lot like the portion of the basement they'd raced through previously—except for the heap of rubble nearby. Thick heating and cooling pipes ran along the walls and ceiling. Oily puddles covered the dirty floor. Dust filled the air.

Through the dust they saw the holes they'd made in the rotting boards above them. Luckily neither Hardy had been hurt. They pushed some pieces of plaster and rotten wood off their legs and stood up.

"Is anybody down here?" Joe called.

"Yes! Help!" came a strangled cry from beyond the rubble.

The Hardys pushed their way through the debris and discovered Lily crouched on the floor. She looked dirty and frightened, and her leg was caught beneath a big section of pipe that had fallen from the wall.

"I think I'm okay, but I'm stuck," she said.

The brothers grabbed the pipe and heaved with all their strength. Slowly they managed to bend the conduit up, and Lily crawled out from under it. "Thanks," she said, brushing the dirt from her hands.

"What are you doing down here?" Frank asked.

"I took a wrong turn somewhere and lost my partner," she said. "We thought we'd have a better chance of winning if we split up. I guess that was pretty stupid."

"Any idea which way is out?" Joe asked.

Lily shook her head.

Frank shone his light toward both ends of the tunnel. "Pushing through that rubble again might be dangerous, but we know there was a bulkhead somewhere in this direction." He pointed in the opposite direction from the way he and Joe had come.

"Let's go," Joe said.

They groped their way through the semidarkness for a long time, but found no sign of the bulkhead leading to the surface.

"Maybe we got turned around when we fell," Joe said.

"Could be," Frank replied. "Wait! Listen!"

They all paused and heard a loud siren coming from somewhere close by.

"This way," Joe said. He sprinted down a corridor that lead toward the sound. Frank and Lily followed.

At the end of the passage they found an ascending stairway. They paused just long enough to make sure the stairs were sturdy, then they ran up and out of a door on the first floor of the warehouse. Once they were out, they found that they weren't too far from where the Hardys had started the event.

Lily's face brightened. "The sound was the Klaxon!" she said. "Bo must have made it to the center of the maze!"

The Hardys' spirits fell, but they tried not to show their disappointment. Lily raced off to find her partner. A few minutes later, Ward Willingham came by to speak to the brothers.

"Where did you disappear to?" he asked. "You were doing really well, then all of a sudden you left the course."

"We heard Lily call for help," Joe said. "We went to find her."

"She'd gotten caught in the underground," Frank added.

Willingham shook his head and sighed. "Boys, I've made quite a few allowances for you in the past, but I'm afraid this is the end. You left course—and even if it was for good reason, your opponents sounded the Klaxon first."

"We left the course to *save* one of our opponents," Joe protested.

"I know," Willingham replied, "and that's a great story. It'll make an interesting side story for the show. You've been great contestants—really great. But the show is about *winning* the competitions, and this time you lost. I can't keep rerunning games on your behalf. I've done that a couple of times already."

"We understand," Frank said, though Joe didn't look as willing to accept defeat. "Come on, Joe. Let's get something to drink."

"That's the spirit," Willingham said. "Watch the rest of the competitions, if you like. Your friends, Morton and Soesbee, are still in the running." He shook hands with both brothers. "Thanks, guys. You can check with Ms. Kendall about your consolation prizes."

"Sure," Joe said glumly.

He and Frank adjourned to the break area and got themselves sodas. The number of people getting refreshments had thinned considerably, since the competition was entering its final stages. They saw Lily and Bo briefly. Lily waved and mouthed the words, "Thank you." Bo grinned like the cat who had eaten the canary.

"Let's go find Chet and Daphne," Joe said, "before I take my anger out on those two."

From the staff the teens discovered that Chet and Daphne's event was being held on the infamous toxic-pool set. They headed in that direction, but ran into Ms. Kendall on the way.

"Sorry to hear you're not advancing," she said sympathetically. "You really livened up the show."

"The show livened up our lives a bit too," Frank replied.

Ms. Kendall gave them their consolation packages: clothing and accessories with the show's logo, discount coupons from local merchants and attractions, and a one-thousand-dollar scholarship bond. She thanked them again, then ran off to her next assignment.

"Pretty good for a couple of days' work," Frank said.

"Nothing to put us on *Lifestyles of the Rich and Spoiled,* though," Joe said.

Loot in hand, they found a convenient spot from

which to watch Chet and Daphne compete. By the time the brothers arrived, the game was nearly over. Chet and Daphne had built a bridge over the pool from scrap metal and other debris that had been strewn around the set. Missy and Jay began putting the final pieces on their own bridge as Chet and Daphne stepped onto their construction.

The Hardys' friends tottered across the rickety apparatus toward the far side of the pool. As they neared the end, Chet lurched and almost lost his footing. For a moment it looked as though he would topple into the bubbling green water.

Missy and Jay stepped onto their makeshift bridge.

As Chet teetered on the brink, Daphne reached out and grabbed his hand. She gave a hard yank and pulled him across the bridge—and over the finish line. A golden band rested on a rusty pedestal nearby.

Chet grabbed it and shouted, "Yes!"

Ward Willingham appeared and congratulated them, then offered his condolences to the losers. Missy and Jay stuck their tongues out and skulked away.

"Class, all the way," Joe said, rolling his eyes.

Since setting up for the finals would take some time, Chet and Daphne had the rest of the afternoon off. The four friends stopped at the Town Spa restaurant to celebrate Chet and Daphne's success. They used one of the Hardys' consolation coupons to pick up some pizzas for cheap, then headed back to the Hardys' home for an early dinner.

"You know," Chet said as they ate around the kitchen table, "I think this is the first time I've finished a contest ahead of you guys."

Frank and Joe laughed. "This time, the better team won," Frank said.

"Yeah," Joe agreed. "I hope that turns out to be true in the finals, too. But someone is definitely messing with *Warehouse Rumble*. And the big question is: Why?"

"Have the problems on the sets been accidents, or are they sabotage?" Frank asked. "Who was lurking around the warehouse with a flashlight the other night? Who was the masked mutant that jumped Chet?"

"How did the dead guy—Joss Orlando—get in the chimney?" Chet added.

"And what, if anything, does his skeleton have to do with the rest of the trouble?" Daphne asked.

"Clark Hessmann and Ms. Allen would both profit if *Warehouse Rumble* goes under," Frank said. "Willingham's publicity-hungry, so the news reports—even when they're bad—might benefit him too. Bo Reid, Jay Stone, and Missy Gates were all helped by the accidents—even though Missy got hurt."

"She seemed okay today, though," Daphne said.

"Right. So we can't rule any of them out as suspects," Frank said.

"If Missy and Jay were the masterminds, it didn't

stop them from being eliminated," Chet noted.

"How does it all tie together?" Joe asked, clearly frustrated.

"How did Ms. Forbeck's ring get in the warehouse?" Daphne asked. "Could someone have planted it there for publicity?"

"The chance of you stumbling on it seems pretty slim, given where it was," Chet said.

"We don't even know how long that ring had been there," Frank said. Then his brown eyes lit up. "Wait a minute! That's something we haven't looked into."

"How long the warehouse has been abandoned?" Joe said, picking up his brother's thought.

"I bet we can find out on the Internet," Daphne suggested. "The *Bayport Journal-Times* has its archives online."

All four of them pushed aside their food and headed for the Hardys' computers. A few moments later both brothers were surfing the Net as their friends looked on and offered advice.

"You were right, Frank," Joe said. "Those warehouses have been closed for more than twenty years. That ring couldn't have gotten dropped by someone who worked there—it wouldn't have just been sitting in a puddle."

"That suggests it was dropped by the thief—and the thief must have been in the building sometime after the robbery," Frank said.

"There're fifteen years between the robbery and now, though," Chet said.

"Yes," Joe replied, "but none of the other jewels have been recovered. The police or insurance company would have spotted them if they'd turned up on the market. If the thief didn't dispose of the jewels, the question is: Why not?"

"Maybe he didn't want to sell them," Chet suggested.

"Why steal them if not to sell them?" Joe asked.

"And if the thief stole them for himself, why lose one in an old warehouse?" Daphne added. "You'd think he'd put them someplace safe."

"You'd *think*," Frank said. "So either he didn't sell them because he was lying low for fifteen years . . ."

" . . . or he didn't sell them because he *couldn't*," Joe said. "Either because he lost them, or . . ."

" . . . because he died shortly after stealing them." Chet blurted. "The skeleton in the chimney!"

"You think Joss Orlando stole the jewels?" Daphne asked.

Both brothers nodded.

"Get a load of this," Frank said, reading from his computer screen. "It's from fifteen years ago: 'Bayport resident Joss Orlando has been missing for over two weeks now. Police are baffled as to his disappearance. His wife and small children haven't seen Mr. Orlando since the night of April sixteenth,

138

when he went out to get some groceries—'"

"April sixteenth!" Chet put in. "That's the night of the Forbeck robbery!"

"Exactly," Frank said. "But there's more." He and the others continued to read silently as Frank scrolled through the rest of the article.

"So," Joe said after they finished reading, "the trouble on the set of *Warehouse Rumble* isn't about the game—it's about the missing jewels."

"Aside from Chet's accident, the real trouble only started after the news broadcast about the skeleton in the chimney," Frank said.

"So the thief was never caught because he was dead in that chimney the whole time," Chet said.

"And the jewels weren't found because he still had them—either in the chimney, or somewhere nearby," Daphne concluded. "Maybe near where I found the ring."

"That seems likely," Frank said, "even though the police searched that tunnel. I'm betting that the lights the exterminator saw in the warehouse came from people who were looking for the jewels."

"But who would even know where to look?" Chet asked.

"They *don't* know where to look," Frank said. "Which is why they're trying to clear everyone out of the warehouse."

"That explains the accidents," Daphne said.

"Here's something else," Joe said, pulling up

another article onscreen. "'Demolition of the warehouse is scheduled to begin next week,'" he read aloud, "'after shooting ends on the show.'"

"So if the jewels are in the warehouse, the thief doesn't have much time to retrieve them," Daphne noted.

"I bet they'll try again tonight," Frank said. "Let's check Orlando's background a bit more, then head down to the warehouse and see what's up."

By the time the Hardys and their friends drove up the dirt road toward the old warehouse, stars were peeking out of the cloudy sky overhead. The *Warehouse Rumble* crew had already departed for the night, and the warehouse complex stood dark and still.

"Look—a light!" Chet said, pointing. "Out on the old docks."

"Joe," Frank said, "turn off the headlights so they don't spot us."

"Check," Joe replied. He switched off the headlights and pulled over as close to the docks as he could without being seen. "Chet, you and Daphne go get the cops while Frank and I check this out."

"I wish we had your cell phone," Daphne said.

"Those are the breaks," Frank replied, shrugging. He and Joe got out of the van. "Come back as quickly as you can. We'll make sure the thief doesn't escape."

"Right," Chet said. "See you in a couple of minutes." He slid behind the wheel and drove back they way they'd come. The Hardys sneaked down toward the old docks.

Knee-high weeds and tangled bracken made traversing the hillside between the road and the docks tricky, but the Hardys' Scout training enabled them to move quickly and almost noiselessly through the brush.

As they drew closer they saw figures moving on the third wharf over.

"I only see one guy," Joe whispered.

"That's surprising," Frank whispered back. "I was expecting two."

The man prowling the docks wore black clothing and a ski mask. He was careful about using his flashlight—but not careful enough. The brothers easily kept track of him as they crept closer. He seemed to be tying a rowboat to one of the pylons.

As the Hardys crept up behind him, someone yelled, "Look out!"

The masked man turned, a big oar in his hand, and rushed toward the brothers.

The oar caught both Hardys in the chest as the thief pushed them toward the edge of the dock. Within seconds the rotten boards gave way beneath their feet, and the Hardys sank to the dark waters below.

15 Dock and Tackle

Frank and Joe both managed to grab the edge of the dock as they went down. Splinters of wood stabbed their hands, but they held on tight. The thief continued swinging his oar at their heads, showing no mercy.

The Hardys ducked, and the burglar missed. His effort nearly sent him over the brink with them. With a snarl, he threw the oar at the brothers, then turned and ran toward the warehouse. The oar missed Frank, but it smashed Joe across the fingers.

Joe yelped and lost his grip on the dock. Frank reached his hand out just in time, and grabbed the back of Joe's shirt. The younger Hardy's feet splashed in the chilly water for a moment before he grabbed on to a nearby pylon.

Just when Joe was in the clear, Frank's remaining fingers slipped off the decaying wood. He thrust his other hand up just in time to prevent himself from falling. With a mighty effort he heaved himself onto the rotten planking once more. Then he stuck his hand down and helped Joe up.

"Thanks," Joe said. "Did you see which way he went?"

Frank edged across the dock and glanced at the boat. "No loot here," he said, "and he wouldn't have had time to collect it before running. I'm betting they're still searching the warehouse for more buried treasure."

"We'd better go after them," Joe said. "They won't try to escape this way now. And you know, they probably stole the rowboat to begin with."

The brothers left the decaying docks and raced toward the warehouse. The heavy chain that locked the back door had been cut. The dilapidated property had no electronic security system, despite the fact that TV sets and expensive equipment were stored inside.

"Lucky for the thieves—and us," Joe noted.

While escaping the wharf, they'd lost sight of the burglar. Fortunately the noise of his movements echoed through the eerie silence of the warehouse. It didn't take the brothers long to home in on the sounds.

They climbed through a bulkhead door and

carefully descended a rickety stairway into the basement. Frank's penlight gave them just enough light to see by.

"Weren't the furnace rooms this way?" Joe whispered.

"That would make sense," Frank whispered back. "A furnace below that broken chimney."

Joe nodded.

"Keep moving!" said a voice echoing through the darkness. "Those guys know we're here! They can't be far behind. They might have even called the cops!"

"I knew they were trouble," a second, higher voice replied. "It's too bad our tricks didn't put them out of commission for good."

Joe held up two fingers and mouthed the word *two* to his brother.

Frank shot him a smile. Their original suspicions had been right.

A light shone out of a doorway on the right side of the dark tunnel ahead. Frank motioned that they should try a flanking maneuver. Joe nodded and pressed himself against the wall opposite the door. He crept quickly to the far side of the door, staying out of the light.

"Give me a hand, here," said the first voice. "The bag is wedged in."

"Cut the bag if you have to," said the second voice. "We only want what's inside."

Joe peeked into the room and then mouthed to Frank, *No way out.*

Guns? Frank mouthed back.

Joe shook his head.

Frank nodded and called, "We know you're in there. The police are on the way. You might as well give up!"

A masked figure charged out of the room toward Frank's voice. He held a sledgehammer, and was clearly looking to pound someone. His eyes narrowed as he spotted Frank.

Quick as a flash, Joe darted out of the shadows and grabbed the thief from behind. He slipped his hands up behind the burglar's neck, locking him in a full-nelson wrestling hold. The sledgehammer slipped from the burglar's grasp and clanked onto the tunnel floor. "Help!" the thief gasped.

A smaller masked figure ran out of the furnace room, crowbar in hand, and headed toward Joe and the struggling burglar.

Frank dropped into a spin-kick and swept the second thief's legs out. The smaller burglar landed hard on the damp concrete floor. Frank pinned the thief to the ground.

Within moments the Hardys had subdued both intruders and tied them with their belts. The sound of police sirens approaching the warehouse echoed through the dank passageway. Frank and Joe looked at each other and grinned.

"Lily and Todd Sabatine, I presume," Joe said.

He and Frank pulled off the intruders' black ski masks.

Todd growled something incoherent; Lily spat at them.

The brothers dusted themselves off and peered into the room that the Sabatines had just exited. Inside lay the rusting hulk of the old furnace at the bottom of the broken chimney. A black leather valise was caught in the iron grating that covered the furnace door.

Rats had eaten several holes in the old case. Even in the dim light of the basement the gold and gemstones inside glittered.

"I'm sure," Frank said, "that Ms. Forbeck will be glad to have her jewels back."

The impromptu celebration at the Hardy house lasted until well after midnight. Callie and Iola had shown up, and the Hardys' parents joined the party too. As they discussed the Hardys' case, Aunt Gertrude continuously replenished the supply of milk and cookies.

"You four sure can get into a lot of trouble without Callie and me," Iola said, smirking.

"Trouble or no," Fenton Hardy said, "you did well. I'm very proud of you both."

"So, Clark Hessmann, Stacia Allen, Bo Reid, and

even Missy and Jay had nothing to do with the problems?" Callie asked.

"Amazingly, no," Joe replied. "They were just being opportunistic. The Sabatines were behind all the trouble."

"The thing that made them hard to catch," Frank said, "was that the two of them worked together."

"For instance, Todd never even went to the cast party," Joe continued, "and that's where Willingham's prescription sleeping pills were dumped into the punch bowl. Lily did that."

"And at other times, Todd would cause trouble while Lily had an alibi," Frank said. "Occasionally they even created alibis for each other, and tried to throw suspicion on someone else."

"Like Bo, or Missy and Jay," Daphne said, "who all were pretty suspicious anyway."

"I guess the Sabatines figured that anything that slowed down the production was helpful to them," Chet said.

"Right," Joe agreed. "They needed time to find the lost jewels. Joss Orlando—the thief—was their father. As we saw in the newspaper archive, their mother remarried after he disappeared, and changed the family name to Sabatine. Todd and Lily were just little kids at the time. Because of that, no one connected them to the skeleton in the chimney. When Todd and Lily heard that their father's body had been discovered, they knew the jewels he had stolen had to be hidden somewhere in the warehouse."

"My police contacts believe the Sabatines' mother knew where Joss Orlando had gone the night he disappeared," Mr. Hardy said. "She knew he was a thief—even though his police record was clean. The story that he went out for groceries and never came back was something she fabricated for the press. She didn't worry at first, because she knew the Forbeck robbery had been successful; it was in every newspaper. But when her husband didn't come back or even call, she reported him as missing. She probably hoped the police would bring him home so she could get her cut. She died a couple of years ago, without ever finding out what had happened to him."

"The Sabatines' mom must have told her kids the truth about their father's disappearance," Frank said. "When Orlando's body turned up, Lily and Todd auditioned for *Warehouse Rumble* just so they could search the warehouse. They appeared late for auditions, remember?"

"So Todd's ankle injury was a sham," Daphne said, nodding.

"Yeah," Joe said. "It allowed him to hang around the set, without having to participate in any of the games. He must have taken the opportunity to both search the warehouse and sabotage some of the games."

"The police found a ketchup-stained sock at the Sabatine house, as well the mutant costume he used to attack Chet," Fenton Hardy added.

"He nearly hurt his sister with that falling-tower stunt," Chet said.

"Clearly, that didn't go quite as they'd planned," Joe said.

"I remember at the time how mad Lily looked," said Daphne.

"That might have gone wrong," Joe said, "but her near-miss did avert suspicion from them. If not for that and his 'injury,' we might have connected Todd with that accident *and* the reappearance of the sleeping pills much earlier. He was responsible for both—though he tried to pin the missing prescription on us. Turns out the falling catwalk was his work too."

"The confusion and the media circus both worked to Todd and Lily's advantage," Frank said. "In all the chaos, no one gave any thought to either of the Sabatines being missing."

"No one but you and Joe," Iola corrected.

"I did think it was strange when we rescued Lily from the cellar," Frank said. "Why was she there? We now think she was searching for the jewels while Bo was continuing with the game. He never suspected he was her alibi."

"She got caught under the pipe by accident," Joe said. "The warehouse is a pretty dangerous place, despite what Willingham wants people to believe. We found her pretty close to where Daphne discovered the Forbeck ring."

"What I wonder," Laura Hardy asked, "is how did Joss Orlando's body end up in that chimney?"

"The police sent some cops out to search for the thief after the robbery," Frank said. "Joss must have hidden in the old warehouse to escape them."

"Forensic tests are already showing that Orlando had numerous broken bones when he died," Fenton Hardy said. "Apparently he fell into the chimney—and that's probably what killed him."

"He must have been up on the roof, trying to escape the police," Joe suggested, "when a portion of the chimney gave way and he fell in."

"Just like it collapsed when I fell against it," Chet said.

"But with more fatal results," Frank noted.

"And the bag with jewels slipped down through the chimney into the furnace below," Callie said. "I guess rubble covered it up until the Sabatines—and Frank and Joe—found it." She sighed. "If only we got to *keep* some!"

"There should be a reward," Fenton Hardy said, "which would surely help your college funds."

"But why wasn't the ring Daphne found with the rest of the treasure?" Iola asked.

"The holes in the leather bag the jewels were stored in give us the answer to that," Frank said.

"We know a lot of rats are living in the warehouse. We saw them the other day, when Todd Sabatine stirred them up with a smoke bomb so the TV crew would flee."

"The holes in the valise containing the jewels were surely chewed by rats," Joe continued. "They pulled out that ring and dragged it to where Daphne found it. It wasn't far from the furnace room—at least not for a crawling rat. Some rats like shiny things."

"And teens like Lily and Todd Sabatine," Chet quipped.

All of them laughed.

"Those kids would have been better off if they hadn't followed in their father's footsteps," Fenton Hardy said.

"It's so sad when young people go wrong," Aunt Gertrude added, arranging some cookies on a plate.

"They'll have a long time to think about their mistakes," Laura Hardy remarked.

"And they'll see it all played back on TV when *Warehouse Rumble* debuts," Iola said.

"With all this publicity," Frank said, "the Sabatines may be catching themselves on reruns for a long time."

"You mean, *we'll* be catching them in reruns," Joe said. They all laughed again.

Daphne let out a long sigh. "I'm beat," she said.

"I don't think I have any energy left to compete in the finals tomorrow!"

"With Lily Sabatine in jail, whom will you compete against?" Iola asked. "Bo Reid is now one teammate short."

"I'm sure Ward Willingham will dig someone up to replace him," Frank said. "He hasn't come all this way just to quit now."

"Of course he'll find a replacement," Chet said. "The TV show must go on!"

She's sharp.

She's smart.

She's confident.

She's unstoppable.

And she's on your trail.

MEET THE NEW NANCY DREW

Still sleuthing,

still solving crimes,

but she's got some new tricks up her sleeve!

NANCY
DREW

girl detective